20p

GW01460184

"What's happening?" Andy asked plaintively.

Mary was too terrified to answer him. Just as she held the boy tight against her with her hands on his shoulder, back to her legs, so the man with the scar had a grip on her. But his was with a forearm locked around her throat, dripping blood from his injured hand on to her dress bodice. In his good hand was a Bowie knife, the point denting the skin of her neck without puncturing it.

"Stick around undertaker!" the killer called as the hearse was pulled to a halt behind the crowd on Jubal's right. "Unless I get what I want, there'll be two more for the cold ground—the lady, and me, I guess. . . ."

THE KILLING TRAIL never ends for Jubal Cade, an idealistic doctor whose dream of beauty and happiness is shattered by the violence of the rugged West. As he watches the ghastly red stain spread on the snow, he acknowledges the grim truth about himself—there is no turning back.

The Killing Trail

Charles R. Pike

CHELSEA HOUSE
New York, London
1980

Chelsea House Publishers
Harold Steinberg, Chairman & Publisher
Andrew E. Norman, President
Susan Lusk, Vice President

A Division of Chelsea House Educational Communications, Inc.
70 West 40 Street, New York 10018

The Killing Trail

CHAPTER ONE

Jubal Cade regarded the city skyline with hope shining in his soft brown eyes. He watched it draw closer for several moments then turned to look for a reaction to the sight from his wife. What he saw caused his expression to cloud and he reached out an arm to encircle her shoulder in a reassuring embrace.

Mary snapped her attention away from the uneven sprawl of buildings across the bleak greyness of the city's harbour and tried to conceal her nervousness behind the thin mask of a smile as she saw the troubled look on Jubal's almost handsome face.

'I'm sorry dear,' she said in her gentle, English-accented voice. 'I really will try not to be afraid of strange places.'

The young man held his wife closer and nodded across the strip of calm water, rapidly narrowing as the brig's canvas billowed in a whispering south-easterly wind to carry the ship towards her berth. 'That's New York, honey,' he said. 'It's got most of the worst and some of the best things London has got. But there's a whole big country on the other side of the city – like nothing you've ever seen.' He smiled and held her slim shoulders in a closer grip. 'Even I'm a little scared of it. But together we can take it on and make every square mile of it our own. Okay?'

Mary nodded energetically and suddenly a deep love blazed in her eyes as she looked into the fervent excitement portrayed on Jubal's face. 'Together, I think we could do anything you wanted, Jubal,' she replied with the degree of assurance befitting a bride of three months.

The couple stayed on the forecastle of *Orion* until her master had brought her skilfully to rest beside an East River quay. Then they hurried below to their cabin to collect their ready-packed baggage and joined the rest of the passengers filing down the gangplank.

Jubal experienced no particular surge of emotion as he stepped on to his native land after an absence of seven years. If he felt anything, it was probably a sense of disappointment that the waterfront had changed so little since he sailed from almost this very spot all those years ago. It was still wretched, half-decayed and filthy, with the aromas of fresh cargoes from every part of the world masked by the stench of older consignments which had spoiled.

As the passengers were hustled roughly into two groups – American nationals and aliens – Mary sensed her husband's mild disenchantment and gave his upper arm an affectionate squeeze.

'Most places look better from a distance, Jubal,' she said, having to raise her voice to be heard above the bellows of customs men and multi-languaged complaints from the bewildered and frightened European passengers. 'When you can't see the scars.'

With both his hands engaged in carrying the four valises, Jubal was unable to offer a physical response and he confined himself to a smile of acknowledgement.

In addition to the couple, there had been five other Americans as passengers on the English brig and this small group was herded into a customs shed with little more regard than was shown towards the aliens.

A sweating, red-faced officer in a dirty uniform jacket raked arrogant eyes over Jubal then showed tobacco-stained teeth in a blatant leer as he surveyed Mary.

'Papers?' he demanded, sticking out a hand towards Jubal but continuing to stare lustfully at the woman.

She was a small, delicately formed woman of twenty, dressed in a grey gown with a high neckline, fitted at the bodice in such a way to hint at, rather than emphasize, the proud thrust of her breasts, narrow waist and finely sculptured hips. Beneath the wide brim of her white bonnet, fine-spun wheat-coloured hair fell in long sweeps to caress her shoulders, framing a face that was as compactly pretty as her

8

body promised to be. She responded to the officer's unconcealed interest with a steady, cool gaze from her deep blue eyes. Her well-formed mouth was compressed into a tight line and her unblemished cheeks showed widening patches of pink against the paleness of her complexion under the unremitting surveillance of the customs man. He was in his fifties, ugly and made uglier by a two-day growth of stubble. He had bad breath.

'It's been a long trip,' Jubal said frostily. 'My wife and I'd like to get to our hotel.'

The customs man took the papers from Jubal, then used his sleeve to wipe a bead of sweat from the tip of his large nose. He transferred his attention back to Jubal and the arrogance of official power re-entered his small eyes. 'If I had a little lady like this for a wife, I'd be kinda anxious to get to someplace private, mister,' he rasped. 'But you'll just have to await my pleasure before you get to yours.'

'Look at the papers,' Jubal instructed.

'What?' His tone became harsher.

'Not mister,' Jubal replied.

The sweating man shuffled through the documents, then looked up with an expression of mock apology. 'Sorry. Doctor.' He did a double-take at the papers, and when he returned his attention to Jubal his insolence was pierced by a stab of mild anxiety. 'Doctor Cade? Chief of Immigration is named Cade?' An inflection of his tone added the queries to his statements. 'Charles Cade?'

'Uncle Charlie,' Jubal said with a mild grin.

When he smiled, Jubal seemed to drop several of his twenty-seven years so that his regular features took on the lines of boyish charm. At five feet six inches, he was only two inches taller than his new wife. And he was almost as slim, but weighed considerably more since he was large-boned and his wiry-looking frame was fleshed with a great deal of hard muscle. Now, as he ceased smiling and surveyed the discomfiture of the officer with a level gaze his full age became apparent again and his face seemed to express a tacit warning that his small stature was backed by innate strength: developed by ample experience. His face was pale, with regular features neatly arrayed beneath close-cropped black hair. The brown eyes were deep set, the cheek bones high, the jawline firm and the mouth full. What prevented it from being handsome was a lack of visual character. One looked at him saw a man, like a thousand others. So that, unless there was a particular reason to notice him, he would never stand out in a crowd.

The customs officer, suddenly sweating more profusely, had a reason to view him with greater interest than he normally showed to the constant stream of disembarked passengers passing through his restricted area of jurisdiction.

'I didn't know Mr. Cade had any brothers or sisters,' the officer said nervously, handing the sheaf of papers back to Jubal and pointedly not looking towards Mary.

Jubal tilted the dark blue derby on to the back of his head and carefully refolded the documents before putting them back into the inside pocket of his black suit jacket. There was a gold chain slung across the front of his matching vest and he hauled out the watch on one end. He snapped open the face cover and saw the time was a quarter after four. He fixed the officer with a cool stare. 'There are two trunks in the *Orion's* hold,' he said, and now it was his turn to avoid looking at Mary, whom he sensed was eyeing him quizzically. 'I reckon Uncle Charlie'd be pleased if you did what you could to speed up the unloading.'

The officer hesitated only a moment, then threw up a grimy hand to touch his cap peak. 'Sure thing, Dr. Cade. You and Mrs. Cade go ahead outside and I'll make sure the rest of your baggage follows right quick, sir.'

Under the envious gazes of his fellow-American passengers, whose valises and carpetbags were being pawed into by sour-faced officers, Jubal hefted his hand-baggage and led Mary out of the fetid shed and into the sunlit bustle of South Street.

'You told me you never had any relatives, Jubal,' Mary accused after glancing through the doorway and seeing the officer hurrying out towards the pier.

'I promised I'd never lie to *you*, honey,' he said with a grin

10

as he set down the valises and beckoned to a hire carriage.

'You mean —?' she started.

He winked at her as the driver climbed down and began to heft the baggage up into the rig. 'Just hope he doesn't run into Charlie Cade before we're long gone, honey.'

Mary swallowed hard and glanced nervously up at the prow of the *Orion* thrusting her bowsprit out over the wharf. 'What if he does?' she asked.

Jubal helped her into the rig and slid on to the seat beside her. 'And I thought you were a girl who always looked on the bright side,' he replied with a laugh.

It was true that she invariably did so, but the kind of life she had lived in a small town in the county of Berkshire, England had ensured that for the most part she was protected from fate's harsher aspects. She was the only daughter of a wealthy surgeon and as such she had led something of a sheltered existence. She met Jubal when her father, under whom the young American was studying in his final year, invited his favourite pupil to dinner at the big country house. Jubal – normally very shy with women – had been attracted to her at once, but it had been a slow, heart-searching experience to discover he was in love with Mary. He had made it more difficult for himself by struggling against his emotions since marriage had no part in his immediate plans. Whereas she had been struck by love-at-first-sight and despite the advice of her father – who knew of the young American's starry-eyed dreams – refused to face the reality of the situation and maintained that her love for Jubal would conquer all.

Spoiled throughout her life by an over-indulgent father, Mary was not about to be refused her most ambitious wish and the marriage was one of the grandest occasions in the county for many years. Aware that Jubal planned to practise medicine far and wide beyond the frontiers of the heavily populated areas of the United States, Mary's father endeavoured to cushion his daughter from some of the physical deprivations in store by offering Jubal a dowry. He declined the offer and Mary supported him in this stand.

'I promised to take him for better for worse, for richer for

11

poorer, Daddy,' she had said to her anxious father. 'I don't care whether we're going to be rich or poor. I just know we're going to be better than better. We're going to be the best.'

'No offence, Jubal,' the old man had responded. 'But isn't she the incurable optimist?'

'Maybe having plenty of hope will make up for some of the things we're missing out on, sir,' Jubal replied.

'Hope doesn't pay the bills, son,' the old man pointed out.

The discussion took place on the day following the wedding and the old man used the term 'son' as if he really did feel a kinship. Jubal appreciated this a great deal, since he had been raised in a Chicago orphanage.

'But it sure helps to have some around when things are looking black,' Jubal answered.

The old man had agreed, and promised the couple that his offer would remain open in case the situation ever became desperate. The following week Jubal received his M.D. and a month later he and Mary sailed for New York.

'There you go, Dr. Cade,' the customs man announced as he emerged from the shed, trailed by two blacks staggering under the weight of the trunks.

Jubal nodded and Mary favoured the man with a wide smile.

'That is really most kind of you,' she enthused, over-playing her gratitude now she was sure Jubal's ploy had worked.

There was not the slightest hint of a leer in the new smile he showed her. 'Great pleasure, ma'am,' he responded.

The rig rocked and sank low on its springs as the heavy trunks were loaded aboard.

'Astor House,' Jubal instructed the driver.

'If you'd care to wait awhile, you're uncle will be here soon, sir,' the officer urged, halting the driver in the process of clucking the horse forward. 'I sent a message you'd come ashore.'

Mary's radiant smile had a sudden, fixed quality about it. As she turned to look at her husband, it cracked at the edges and her lower lip began to tremble. Jubal leaned forward to look across her and now it was his turn to inject a degree of the lascivious into his grin.

'We were only married just before we boarded,' he lied, then compounded it. 'And my wife was sea-sick the entire voyage.'

He winked and Mary gasped and blushed scarlet.

'I'm sure your uncle will understand,' the officer said, giving a wink of his own. 'The Astor, you say? I'll tell Mr. Cade to hold off visiting you until the morning, sir.'

'Oh, at least until then,' Jubal said, and signalled to the driver that he could start.

'Have yourself an enjoyable time in New York, ma'am,' the customs officer called after the departing rig.

'You beast!' Mary hissed, and jabbed the point of her elbow into Jubal's rib.

'Make it the Fifth Avenue Hotel,' Jubal called up to the driver as they turned on to Market Street.

'Astor'll be quieter for newlyweds, mac,' the driver answered.

'We are not newlyweds!' Mary protested. 'We have been married for almost three months.'

The driver glanced over his shoulder in time to see Jubal hug Mary to him in a close embrace and kiss her passionately, silencing further denials. He spat vocally down into the street.

'Looks like the novelty ain't yet worn off for him, ma'am,' he growled.

CHAPTER TWO

The six-storey, marble-fronted hotel was acknowledged as the best in New York. It was also the most expensive and, as such, its luxury was far in excess of what Mary had expected. The moment the bell-boy and porters left them alone in their top floor suite, she tackled Jubal about this.

'You're not going to try to lie your way out of paying the bill for all this?' she asked anxiously, waving an elegant hand to encompass the salon and bedroom leading off.

Jubal turned on his boyish grin. 'Honey, what do you take me for?' he asked, and then his expression became earnest. 'We looked like having trouble down on the waterfront. And I'm prepared to go to almost any length to get out of trouble. That goes twice over now I've got you to take care of. We can afford to stay here for the one night we need, so there'll be no trouble with the bill.'

'But what will we have left over when you've paid, Jubal?' she wanted to know, anxious to put all her trust in him again but concerned by the new facet of his character she had seen at the pier.

'Enough for a wagon, a team and supplies,' he replied with a shrug. 'After that I'll need to start collecting on the time I invested over the past seven years.'

'Jubal, you didn't have to —'

Again he silenced her with a kiss, but this time it was merely a brushing together of their lips and he held her only gently. Then he drew his face away from hers by only an inch and responded to her anxious gaze with a look of earnestness in his own eyes. 'Honey, I did warn you that in the kind of places I want to go, life would be tough and could get rough. I just want you to see that in this country you can be as comfortable as you ever were back home. So that any time you want to, you can have —'

Now it was her turn to silence him and she extricated an arm from between their bodies and placed three fingers gently against his lips.

'I told you, Jubal,' she whispered. 'I've utterly forgotten Daddy's offer. Where you go, I'll go, too. And I promise not to nag you again.'

He kissed her fingers and grinned, holding her out at arms length. 'Is that what nagging is?' he asked. 'The guys at med school warned me I'd have to get used to that part of being married. They made it sound real painful. But it didn't hurt a bit.'

'Oh, you!' she laughed. 'When are we going to eat? I feel so empty inside, it's almost as if I had been sea-sick the whole way over.'

'You're just trying to make my stories sound true,' he said.

'The way things are going, I think that's going to be one of my main duties as a wife,' she responded good-naturedly.

They had dinner in the large, talk-filled dining room on the hotel's second floor and Mary was not so hungry as she thought she was. Although she had never, in fact, been sick during the Atlantic crossing, she had not been the best of sailors and the storms which hit the brig towards the end of the voyage had drained her of a lot of energy.

'Early night, honey?' Jubal suggested.

'Would you mind?'

'If you don't mind being alone for a couple of hours,' he replied. 'I'll fix up the wagon tonight and we can get an early start tomorrow.'

She agreed with a sleepy nod, and had to stifle a yawn. 'If you let me have the room key, I'll go up alone,' she offered.

'Something I have to get, honey,' he told her.

The Fifth Avenue was the first hotel in the country to instal an elevator and the uniformed operator hauled the couple up to the top floor. Mary went immediately into the bathroom off the bedroom to brush her teeth, while Jubal started to unfasten the straps on his cabin trunk. When he lifted the lid the trunk's contents showed signs of the violent storm which had plagued

15

the latter part of the voyage. Jubal did not possess a great deal of clothing but that part of his wardrobe not needed aboard the *Orion* had been carefully washed, pressed and folded by Mary for him to pack away. It was still clean, but had been tossed and crumpled and now lay in disarray in the bottom of the trunk. Anxiously, he delved his hands in amongst the shirts, underwear and two suits, and drew out a long, narrow bundle tied with cord at both ends and in the centre.

'What's that?' Mary asked from the bedroom doorway as he worked on the knots.

'Present from the only friend I ever had,' he replied sadly, releasing the final knot and dropping the hessian wrapping back into the trunk. He held out the rifle towards her, but she took a step backwards into the bedroom, a nervous gasp hissing from her lips. 'Thirty calibre Spencer repeating rifle,' he said. 'The Burnside Rifle Company made 35,000 of them during the War Between the States. They all started out as carbines, but I had a rifle barrel conversion made on this one.'

Mary shivered, as if hit by a sudden snap draught. 'I hate guns, Jubal.'

'They're necessary, honey,' he replied, checking the gun and satisfying himself that the buffeting within the trunk had caused no damage. 'Not all the time, but sometimes.'

He re-wrapped the rifle in its protective covering but did not bother with the cords, then rested it back in the trunk. He delved through the crumpled clothing again.

'What happened to your friend?' Mary asked. 'You said *had*.'

'He was killed at Sayler's Creek, Virginia,' Jubal replied. 'Last battle before Lee surrendered at Appomattox Court House. He was a Union infantry captain. He was raised in the same orphanage as I was, so he had no one. He'd told one of the other officers that if anything happened to him, I was to get his personal effects. He must have bought the Spencer, because I got it along with his other stuff. There wasn't much.'

'That, too?' Mary asked.

She was referring to Jubal's second find among the heap of clothes – a three-inch barrel ·41 calibre Remington under-and-over – which he unwrapped from a silk cravat.

He shook his head and smiled. 'No. I won it off another student at med school. Poker.'

She didn't say anything for several moments, watching as Jubal made a further exploration of the trunk and came up with a wooden box. Inside was ammunition for both the Spencer and the Remington. He broke the tiny handgun and loaded both barrels, then dropped a half dozen rimfire cartridges into a side pocket of his jacket.

'Tonight's one of the times, Jubal?'

He eyed her quizzically.

'That you'll need a gun,' she amplified.

'I hope not, honey,' he replied, moving across to her, his face breaking out with the boyish grin. 'But New York's no quiet English country village. Don't worry, honey.' He dropped the gun into his pants' pocket and patted the slight bulge. 'The gun's to keep me out of any trouble that might come up. Not get me into it.'

She moved into his arms and he held her face in his hands as he kissed her. She could smell the gun oil on his fingers. 'Come back soon,' she pleaded.

'Don't blink, honey,' he told her cheerfully, tapping her under the chin with a knuckle. 'If you do, you won't even know I've been gone.'

He re-crossed the room to the door. 'Take care, Jubal,' Mary called after him.

'If I ever needed a better reason to do that, you're it,' he replied with a grin as he went out into the hallway.

Downstairs, the reception hall was noisy with sounds filtering from the dining room and bar and outside, beyond the marble porch of the hotel, Fifth Avenue was bustling with evening traffic. Jubal stood under the canopy for several moments, watching the throng of strollers on the sidewalk and the line of carriages, street cars and stages moving on the street. He recalled how, seven years ago, he had found New York such an exciting place to wait out the three days and nights before the clipper sailed to England.

But now, as he took time to test his reactions, nothing of

17

that youthful feeling came back to him. In fact, he experienced the same lack of emotion that had been with him when he stepped off the brig. And it did not surprise him as he moved into the throng of strollers, turning south on Fifth Avenue then angling across to Broadway. For New York was not the America he had come home to: just as Chicago, the city of his childhood and youth held no strings on his heart. His ambitions lay much further west: precisely where he had yet to discover, for that half of the country on the far side of the Mississippi was just a dream conjured up by his own imagination from the books he had read during the precious spare time between studies in England.

He had read both good and bad about the West and had relied upon his own commonsense to differentiate between the fact and the fiction. What had emerged from it all was something which Jubal himself termed a hankering – nothing more than an overwhelming desire to penetrate the dream and discover the realities.

This evolved before he met Mary and so deeply was he smitten by love for her that he had been prepared to set aside his very personal ambition had she wanted a different future. But her love for him equalled his for her and it was a serious condition of her acceptance of his proposal that his plans should remain unaltered.

Jubal continued walking south on Broadway to Union Square, then turned east on 17th Street. He knew precisely where he was headed and quickened his pace, the thoughts of Mary making him anxious to return to her. The address of a wagon trader on Third Avenue had been given him by one of the seamen on the *Orion*. The sailor had a reputation for knowing exactly where to get the best for the cheapest price in New York – from a girl for the night to a diamond necklace in case a man's wife found out about the whore. He ran his information service in a businesslike manner, to the extent that he had cards printed with his name which introduced customers to suppliers and ensured he received commission on the deals.

After the gaslit brightness of Broadway, the square and 17th

Street beyond were very dark. The street was flanked for the most part with business premises, shuttered and silent. The new moon was low in a thinly clouded sky so that one half of the street was in heavy shadow, with the opposite sidewalk patched by blue luminescence. Jubal walked slowly along in the shadows, checking for street numbers. When he spotted one and realized he had several blocks to cover before reaching the wagon dealer, he quickened his pace.

'What's your hurry, Dr. Cade?'

Jubal had thought he was alone on the street, since the only sound against the background hum of the great city was the click of his own heels on the paved sidewalk, echoing back at him from the façades of the buildings. He halted abruptly and looked back over his shoulder, instantly recognizing the voice of the customs man. The street seemed as empty as before, with nobody silhouetted against the distant brightness of the intersection with Broadway.

'Got nothing to say for yourself?'

Jubal pinpointed the man's position – on the other side of the street in a doorway about sixty feet away. 'Didn't I declare enough at the customs shed?' he called in reply.

The big man stepped out into the moonlight. He had changed out of his uniform into a suit that looked no cleaner. He was still sweating. His teeth shone in a sly smile and he hooked his thumbs in his pants' pockets as he leaned casually against an upright supporting the porch canopy.

'You sure had plenty to say for yourself,' the man said easily. 'Made a fool of me.'

Jubal had spent a great deal of his childhood behind the brown stone walls of the Chicago orphanage. But he had been allowed out on the streets sometimes. What he had learned in the outside world at a young age had stood him in good stead when he started work. A lot of people – boys and men – had made the mistake of assuming his small stature meant weakness. One of the early lessons he had learned was to accept nothing at face value. Fear everything – especially the unknown – until you've beaten it was a tenet that had saved his pocketbook, and sometimes his life, on more than one occasion.

19

'Guess I should have slipped him a couple of bills over the fare,' Jubal said easily, raking his eyes along both sides of the street as he turned around.

The customs man was over-confident: maybe because he thought he could take Jubal with one hand tied behind his back. Then again, maybe he had some help at hand.

'Wouldn't have done you any good, doc,' the big man said, straightening up and ambling across the sidewalk. 'I decide which drivers work off my pier. Didn't take much persuading to find out you'd changed your mind about a place to stay. Stan! Jimmy!'

As he stepped down on to the street and called their names, two men emerged from an opposite doorway, on the same side as Jubal. They appeared as just two shadowy human forms against the darkness of the night. Both were tall and broad but, like the customs man, light on their feet.

'All I had to do then was wait for you to show. Kinda hoping the little lady would be with you.'

As he spoke, he continued to move slowly towards Jubal. The other two waited until he was level with them, then fell in beside him, matching his casual pace.

'Got you in bad with your boss, uh?' Jubal asked easily, allowing his hands to hang loosely at his sides.

'He weren't happy,' the customs man replied. 'Reckoned as how you might have pulled that trick so I wouldn't check your baggage. What you bring in, doc?'

He, and the others, halted about ten feet in front of where Jubal stood. In unison, as if they had rehearsed it carefully, each man thrust his right hand into his jacket pocket.

'Should have asked me back at the pier,' Jubal answered. 'Reckon that now I'm off the waterfront and you're out of uniform, it's no longer any of your business.'

'We come here to talk or what?' one of the other men demanded sourly. He drew a hand from his pocket and the brassy shine of knuckle dusters was caught by the moonlight.

The customs man gave an angry grunt. 'If I can hang something on this guy, Charlie Cade'll have to eat some of the cuss words he tossed at me.'

'That weren't part of the deal, Ed,' the other helper complained. His hand came out of his pocket empty, but delved under his jacket to haul out a short wooden club.

Jubal felt the sweat begin to pump, pasting his shirt to his back and making his palms sticky. He pressed his arms close to his sides and his wrists rested against the bulging pockets of his jacket. In one was his bankroll – enough to pay the hotel bill and buy the necessities for a trip west. In the other was the more solid bulk of the Remington and its spare ammunition.

'How much is he paying you for this?' Jubal asked.

'That's *our* business,' the helper on the left barked.

'Good business to bargain,' Jubal suggested.

'Get the bastard!' Ed yelled.

Stan and Jimmy looked at each other, unwilling to make the first move.

'Twenty bucks apiece,' one of them said.

'Double it to beat it,' Jubal suggested in the same easy tone, unaware of exactly how they would react: sure only that there could not possibly be a deal. For they had to go on living in the same city as Ed who was proving himself not a man to be trifled with.

But the men used up valuable seconds in looking at each other again and Ed stared angrily at both of them. Within a fraction of a second of each other, both men realized what Jubal's words meant – he was carrying at least forty dollars which could be added to the fee Ed was paying them. They swung their heads to look at Jubal, and got as far as raising their legs to take a step towards him. But Jubal had put the pause to good use and was gripping the tiny Remington, aiming it at Ed's bulbous stomach.

'Jesus, you didn't say nothin' about any gun, Ed,' the man on the right muttered.

Ed forced a laugh. 'Hell, that little thing wouldn't hardly make a hole through paper!' he derided. But he held his place in the three-man line.

Jubal showed his boyish grin. 'Why don't you fellers turn around and go back home,' he said.

'Another time, Ed?' one of the helpers said, starting to turn.

21

'Stay where you are!' Ed snarled. 'You too, Stan! I'm goin' for him. Even if he hits me with that toy gun, it won't hardly make a dent. You grab him.'

As he spoke the final word, he launched himself forward, his hand springing free of his pocket. The short-bladed throwing knife spun across the gap in a powerful, underarm trajectory. Jubal had been watching the concealed hand and started his own move the moment Ed's arm began to bend at the elbow. He altered the aim of the under-and-over and threw himself down into a crouch. The knife whistled over his head and Ed's massive form towered above him. Frustration showed on the sweating face of the man as the knife glanced off the front of a building and clattered to the sidewalk. But then an evil grin spread across his features as he added impetus to his forward momentum, hands reaching out for a stranglehold. He started to fall forward on to the crouching man.

Jubal rocked backwards, off his haunches. He sat down and rolled on to his back, his legs still bent at the knees. Timing the move to perfection, he sprang his legs out straight, thrusting them into the air. His heels thudded powerfully into Ed's belly and the stinking wind burst out of the big man's lips. Jubal had placed the two-footed kick well and altered the direction of the thrust at precisely the right moment. The gasping Ed was lifted bodily off his feet and tipped into an ungraceful somersault over Jubal's smoothly moving form. He hit the sidewalk with a solid, bone jarring impact, head, torso, arms and legs making simultaneous contact. But even while he was still in midair, Jubal had snapped into a sitting position, legs splayed out in front of him, the Remington aimed with rock steadiness between the advancing Stan and Jimmy. Both men were halted in their tracks, their weapons held in midswing. Behind Jubal, the ragged, pained breathing of Ed indicated there would be no danger from that direction for some time.

'Deal's off, fellers,' Jubal said. 'Nothing to beat it.'

Stan and Jimmy eyed each other nervously, then glanced around Jubal towards Ed.

'What about him?' Jimmy asked.

Jubal got carefully to his feet, picking up his derby with his free hand and setting it back on his head. He sidestepped to the front of an office building, from where he could see all three of them again. Ed was clutching at his middle and groaning. Blood was matting his hair from a split bruise on the back of his head.

'He needs a doctor,' Jubal said.

'You're a doctor,' Stan pointed out.

Jubal grinned. 'He doesn't seem to be responding too well to my kind of treatment. Pick him up and haul him out.'

Both men hurriedly thrust their weapons back into their respective resting places and moved forward, stooping to lift Ed, one taking his feet, the other his shoulders. The injured man's pain-glazed eyes regarded Jubal with naked hate as he was raised from the sidewalk. Blood dripped from his head wound to splash on the paving stones.

'Like Jimmy said, another time!' he rasped.

'Sure, feller,' Jubal told him as he was carried off towards the lights of Broadway, the men's soft-soled city shoes making hardly any noise as they staggered with their burden. 'I like operating on the hard cases.'

CHAPTER THREE

His parting comment to the customs man was not true. Although during his early years he had found it necessary to do more than his fair share of fighting to maintain his dignity – and on occasion to survive – he had an innate hatred of violence. And his choice of medicine as a career, which all this meant in terms of dedication to the preservation of human life, was a natural extension of how he felt towards his fellow men. But although he harboured high ideals, he was also a realist. Ideals were practical only in a perfect world and he had good reason to know that the one in which he lived fell far short of perfection. Thus, the lessons he had learned in Chicago street fights and bar-room brawls were as well remembered as those taught him in the hospital wards and classrooms of far off England. So that each body of knowledge was ready to be called upon, according to the circumstances which were presented to him. He had derived no more enjoyment from knocking the steam out of the customs man than if he had been required, instead, to lift a bullet from a vital organ of the same victim. Both were useful techniques to know in an imperfect world. Neither were pleasant acts, but to complete either successfully gave a man such as Jubal a sense of satisfaction.

So he was content, rather than exhilarated, as he continued east along 17th Street, kicking Ed's throwing knife into the gutter as he reached where it lay. The building bearing the number which the sailor had given him presented the same darkened face to the street as its neighbours. But Jubal had been assured it was in order to call at any time, day or night. The doorway showing the number was not, in fact, on the street. It was a few feet into a wide alley, in the side of a three storey brownstone building. At the front, the ground floor had been a store at one time, but the display window had been

24

masked with black paint. There was a one piece wood door at the front, but it was painted with a faded sign directing callers to use the side entrances. Nowhere was there any indication of the kind of business carried on within the building.

Jubal rapped his fist hard against the panel of the side door and heard a man's voice call that he was coming. Feet shuffled over bare board on the far side, then halted. An old man's wheezing breath sounded.

'Who's there?' came the demand.

'Name's Jubal Cade.'

'Don't mean nothing to me.'

'Guy named Griggs sent me.'

'Should have given you somethin'. Slip it under the door.'

Jubal dug the sailor's card from his vest pocket and pushed it through the crack at the foot of the door. A match was struck and a strip of light marked the crack. The wheezing continued uninterrupted for several seconds, then a bolt was shot back and the door swung inwards. The man was old and stooped, painfully thin with white hair and skin of the appearance of ancient yellowed paper.

'What you want?' he asked, his eyes narrowing to peer suspiciously over the threshold at his visitor.

'You sell other things besides wagons?'

'What I ain't got, I can most always get, mister. You want a wagon?'

'And team.'

The old man jerked his head and Jubal entered. The building smelled, but the old-timer carried a worse stink.

'You sell soap?' Jubal asked as he followed the old man down a hallway and around a right angle turn into another.

'Got a big stock of that,' he said as he halted his shuffling gait before another door and worked a bolt.

'Figured you might have,' Jubal said, welcoming the clean freshness of the night air laced with the smell of stables as he was led out into a yard behind the building.

'You want some?'

'I don't,' Jubal answered.

The old man shrugged and waved the lamp towards a corner

25

of the cluttered yard. 'Only one I got in stock right now, mister. Hundred dollars and she's yours.'

Jubal showed no enthusiasm as he took the kerosene lamp from the old man and moved over for a closer look at the wagon. It was a covered freight – old but with three new wheels and a new canvas. The axles were in good shape and the hubs were well greased. The bed and sides were scratched and gouged, but the wood showed no sign of rot. When Jubal jumped down after his lengthy examination he showed an expression of disapproval.

'Figure fifty,' he said ruefully.

The old man brushed his hands down the front of his tattered and filthy clothing. 'Do I look like I work on a high-profit margin, mister?'

'Seventy-five, so I can sleep at nights,' Jubal offered.

The old man's smile was toothless. 'You got a deal.'

Jubal was then shown six horses and picked the strongest-looking two. He offered what he considered a fair price for the team and it was accepted. He suspected the wagon had been stolen but thought the animals had been obtained honestly. After he had purchased some brand new harness, he received two crumpled dollar bills change from a hundred and twenty. The old man helped him to hitch the team and Jubal's suspicions were strengthened by the dealer's haste in opening the big gates on to the alley and the speed with which they were closed when he had driven through.

Jubal kept a careful eye on each shadowed doorway he passed on the trip back along 17th Street and cast frequent glances over his shoulder. But if the customs man had been serious in his threat of another attack he was apparently going to take the time to lick his wounds first. There was a livery two blocks along 23rd Street from the Fifth Avenue Hotel and Jubal left the wagon and team there, then went up in the elevator to join Mary. He carefully brushed his suit clean of 17th Street sidewalk dust before letting himself into the suite.

Sweet relief showed on Mary's face as she rose from the sofa to greet him. The long wave of hair on the right side of her face was tangled and this told Jubal how anxious she had been

26

while he was out. For Mary had an unconscious habit of toying with her hair when she was worried.

'You got it, Jubal?' she asked, moving close to him and tilting her head to be kissed.

He obliged her. 'We'll just need some supplies when the stores open, then we'll be all set,' he told her.

'No problems?' she asked, eyeing him levelly.

'Missing you was the hardest part,' he replied, evading the issue, recalling the many occasions he had promised never to lie to her.

Her pretty face lit with a smile.

Downtown, the old man shuffled along the hallway again, in response to the thud of a fist against the panel on the side door.

'Who's there?' he wanted to know, a match held close to the wall, ready to strike.

'You Reed the Weed?' a voice asked harshly.

'Guy who sent you ought to have give you something. Slip it under the door.'

There were a few moments of silence, filled only by the wheezing breath of the old man. Then there was a sudden, very loud thud. As the powerful kick crashed against the wooden door, the bolt bracket was torn loose from the frame. The edge of the door slammed into the thin chest of the old man and sent him staggering backwards, knocking him to the floor. The lamp was hurled from his grasp and shattered against the wall. Spilled kerosene splashed over his head and shoulders. The spirit stung his eyes and he rubbed at them frantically. He looked up through his pain and saw a giant of a man silhouetted in the doorway against the pale, filtered moonlight.

'Guy who sent me, sent only me,' the caller announced, stepping across the threshhold. 'Tried to get under the door, but gap weren't wide enough.'

He was six feet six inches tall and carried two hundred and fifty pounds of solid weight. As the old man's vision cleared and the newcomer moved in from the doorway, a gasp interrupted the wheezing breath.

'Luke Travers!' the old man croaked.

One of Travers' massive hands reached down, bunched at the centre of Reed's shirt front and the old man was abruptly jerked upright and thudded against the wall. He was held there, knowing that if the grip was released, his legs would be unable to support him.

'Heard of me, uh?'

Reed gulped and nodded, his smarting eyes staring fearfully into Travers' scowling face across a distance of less than three inches. The big man had a round, smooth-skinned face with a button nose, small mouth and widely spaced, bright blue eyes. He did not look tough and in repose his features seemed to be apologizing for his great bulk. But there were few men on the wrong side of the law in New York who were unaware that, as Boss Egan's top enforcer, Luke Travers was so hard he was almost not human.

'Yessir, Mr. Travers!' Reed croaked. 'And it sure worries me that you're here.'

The big man's bland face adopted the lines of a pleasant smile. 'That's good,' he said. 'Means I don't have to waste no time slapping you around to scare you. Just show me where the wagon is and I'll kill you so it won't hurt.'

'Jesus!' Reed managed to gasp before his teeth began to chatter and his body to twitch.

Travers sighed and his voice took on a complaining tone. 'Hell, ain't no good if you're too scared to talk, Reed. Stay here and I'll look for myself.'

Reed could not control a single trembling muscle in his frail body. Travers pushed him high up the wall in a straight-arm lift, then released his grip on the old man's shirt front. Reed slid down fast, halted abruptly and emitted a high, thin scream. Travers' unbent his knee from between Reed's legs and the old man crumpled to the kerosene-soaked floor, clawing both hands at his crotch.

Travers' bulk moved away from him down the hallway and out of sight around the right angle turn. Reed was engulfed in a sickening sea of pain, but the terror yet to come unlocked his memory and allowed reason to reveal why he was suffering. He'd bought the wagon and team in good faith from a man

28

who needed a fast twenty bucks. The deal was too good for a man like Reed to pass up. Even when the team was sold for fifty cents for slaughter and the harness burned, Reed had been able to fit a new canvas and three new wheels from stock and still make a good profit. How was he to know that the wagon had been stolen from the Egan Interstate Freight Line? Whatever signs had been painted on the sides were sanded off by the time he bought the wagon.

'We heard it was out back today,' Travers said as he reappeared, towering over the crumpled form of the pain-wracked Reed. 'You made a fast deal, Reed. Who bought it?'

The old man tried to press himself closer to the stinking floor as he stared at the highly-polished toecaps of Travers' boots. 'I didn't know it belonged to Boss,' he whined. 'You think I'd —'

'Boss don't pay me to think,' Travers cut in, leaning against the wall, his boots crushing broken glass from the lamp. 'Who bought it and when?'

'Young guy, less than an hour ago,' Reed answered quickly. 'Don't know him. Didn't talk like no New Yorker. Brought a card from an English seaman named Griggs on the *Orion*.'

'We know about your tout, Reed,' Travers said dully and gave another sigh. 'Looks like I'm gonna have to do some leg work.'

More splinters of glass were ground to powder under the enormous weight as Travers stepped over Reed and started towards the still open door. Reed's pain was swamped by a surge of exhilaration. Travers' threat to kill him had been just words. It wasn't true that to cross up Boss Egan meant a man signed his own death warrant. Travers was content with giving the miscreant an agonizing rupture.

'I'll be real careful in the future, Mr. Travers!' the old man called, twisting his head around to look towards the departing giant.

'What future?' Travers asked softly.

Horror cut deep lines into Reed's face as he saw what the big man was doing. The match flared against the wall and the shadows retreated from the dangerous light.

'Please?' the old man begged, rolling on to his back and dragging his hands away from the source of his pain to clasp them in an attitude of prayer.

'Been handling hot stuff too long, Reed,' Travers accused. 'About time you got burned.'

The flaring match arced through the air and an evil-smelling flame shot up from a pool of kerosene, driving the frightened shadows further away. Reed tried to scuttle after them, but the fire was too fast for him. It streaked hungrily along a trickling path of kerosene and made a violent attack on Reed's sopping shirt front. He screamed once, before the flames raced over his face and took a searing grip on his soaked hair. The cloying stench of burnt flesh swamped the old man's body odour.

Travers whistled tunelessly as he crossed the alley, climbed into his buggy and slapped the reins to start the horse forward. The animal was anxious to get away from the wisps of smoke trailing from the side entrance of the building. And by the time Boss Egan's enforcer reached Broadway, the fire glow from far down on 17th Street made the bright gaslights seem pale by comparison.

The big man halted his buggy to allow the racing fire wagons to hurtle past before heading down Fourth Avenue and on to the Bowery. He put the word out from a bar-room on the corner of Bayard and drank beer in a booth until the information began to filter back to him. It took a long time but he liked beer and his enormous frame could absorb a lot of it without ill effect. It was certainly a pleasanter way to pass the night than to personally leg it to Griggs, to Ed and finally to the driver who had taken Dr. and Mrs. Cade to the Fifth Avenue Hotel.

With Travers' powers of persuasion in direct use, the final piece of information would have undoubtedly come from the customs man. But it didn't matter. Boss Egan's organization was as rich in time as it was in money. Provided the result was satisfactory, it could afford to wait.

The sun was well clear of the Atlantic Ocean, promising the city another hot day, when Luke Travers listened to the whispered words of a lisping barfly and hauled himself out of the booth. He did not leave immediately, but first went into a back room to shave. Boss wouldn't like one of his men to enter the plush Fifth Avenue Hotel looking like a bum.

CHAPTER FOUR

The morning sky was still pricked by diamond bright stars when Jubal drove the wagon out of the livery and turned the corner on to the empty avenue, halting level with the hotel's main entrance. Mary sat sleepily on the box seat as a bright-eyed young porter helped Jubal load the luggage into the rear.

Dawn broke rapidly then, with a dull greyness that attacked the night from the east, advancing and brightening by the moment to turn out the starlight in preparation for the sun's arrival. The leading arc of the sun broke clear of the horizon as Jubal manoeuvred the big wagon on to the Weehawken ferry and by the time the heavily-laden side-wheeler had thrashed across the North River to the New Jersey shore the new day was full born.

Mary's tiredness evaporated with the last remants of night and she sat close to Jubal on the high seat, clasping his arm as her gaze swung from left to right, ravenously drinking in the first sights of the enormous spread of country stretching thousands of miles to the west of the city.

'It's beautiful, Jubal,' she enthused when the final vestiges of Jersey City were behind them and the air was fresh and clear, filled with the fragrances and sounds of nature virtually unsullied by man.

'Better than England?' Jubal asked with his boyish grin.

She considered this for a moment, then with a laugh: 'Bigger,' she allowed.

Jubal's desire to leave New York behind and move as soon as possible out into the America he really wanted to see meant they were on their way long before most of the city's stores were open. So they made a breakfast stop at a small farming town many miles down the Pennsylvania Turnpike and Jubal spent almost everything he had left from his bankroll at the dry goods store.

'Goodness,' Mary exclaimed when they were on their way again after she had watched in awe as the supplies were loaded on to the wagon. 'You bought enough to feed an army, Jubal.'

He smiled at her innocence. 'Independence, Missouri's an awful long way, honey,' he said. 'I'm not sure we even have enough to reach there. And Independence is only the start. More than half the country's west of there.'

Mary gulped and raised a hand to her lips as she looked around at the neatly fenced fields richly filled with ripening wheat and verdant green vegetables in the bright sunlight. 'Much bigger,' she whispered in awe, clutching Jubal's arm again, as if the very enormity of the country frightened her.

The morning became hotter as it grew older and by an hour past midday both Jubal and Mary were feeling the effects of the early start to the journey. The last town they had driven through was many miles behind them and the turnpike was winding through low hill country of lush, untilled meadows featured with swathes of undulating timber. The sparkle of water ahead and to the north held out the promise of a pleasant place to rest and refresh themselves and Jubal tugged on the reins to strike the two-horse team away from the turnpike. Although the ground was hard after many days of sun, the iron rims of the wheels left twin trails of broken and crushed grass in the wake of the wagon.

The water was in the form of a small lake with a shoreline of less than a mile around. For the most part it was surrounded by mixed timber which grew to the very edge of the water. But the gap through which Jubal had seen the water's sparkle was more than wide enough to park the wagon and allow both the horses and Mary and himself to enjoy a temporary camp without overcrowding.

While Jubal built a fire, Mary explored the cartons and drums of supplies in the rear of the wagon and collected together the makings of a simple meal in keeping with the heat of the day. They ate it, finishing with fresh apples and coffee while the horses chomped contentedly at the sweet grass in the shade of a beech tree.

'Jubal?' Mary posed when the dishes had been washed, dried and stacked away in the wagon.

'Honey?'

'The water looks fine. Do we have time for a swim? All that time on the ocean and I wasn't even able to trail my hand in it.'

He grinned. 'I reckon, honey. Good day for it.'

She gave a squeal of delight, her hands reaching for the buttons at the back of her dress. But as the gown began to slip from her shoulders, she clutched her arms to her breasts, keeping herself covered. 'What if somebody comes along?' she asked, aghast, glancing hurriedly about her, at the trees, the lake and the low brow of a grassy rise that obscured the turnpike.

Jubal laughed, and the sound was very loud in the stillness of the hot day. 'Anyone came within a mile of here, I figure we'd hear them, Mary,' he assured her.

She looked about her once more, then allowed the gown to fall about her ankles, stooping to remove the frothy underwear. Jubal eyed her slim body with pride, noting with surprise how just the morning drive had added colour to her face: almost brown against the paleness of her nudity.

'Aren't I shocking?' she trilled, turning and loping on her long, slender legs to the water's edge. Then, gracefully, with her body arched and arms held above her head, hands pressed together, she dived in.

She entered the lake surface with hardly a splash and launched into a smooth, fast crawl, her course arrow-straight for the far bank. Jubal watched her for long moments, very conscious of his inability to swim and contemplating the idea of stripping off his own clothes and plunging his sweat-tacky body into a shallow section of the lake. But he decided against it and contented himself with shedding only his jacket and necktie, unfastening his shirt at the collar. He transferred the Remington from the jacket pocket to the waistband of his pants and dropped the loose shells into a vest pocket. Then he climbed into the rear of the wagon, lifted the lid of his trunk and took out the Spencer and ammunition case. He loaded the rifle and rested it against the back of the seat.

When he jumped down to the ground, Mary was within a

few strokes of the bank. Her feet found the lake bed and she stood up, her finely formed breasts rising and falling unhurriedly beneath the crystal clear water. He experienced a swell of desire for her, but didn't dare voice his need. He was afraid that, although she had taken to the water nude with only a token show of modesty, to put his thoughts into words would shock her.

'Goodness, it's even better than it looks, Jubal,' she called. 'Is there time for me to go over and back again?'

'Sure,' he allowed. 'Take me that long to hitch up the horses.'

As she showed him her most loving smile and started to turn, the sharp report of a pistol shot vibrated the hot stillness. Mary became rooted to the soft mud of the lake bed. Jubal whirled around, staring over the backs of the grazing horses towards the hillock separating the lake from the turnpike. Men's voices, far off and raised in excitement, floated across the countryside in the wake of the shot. Then hoofbeats – drawing closer.

Jubal stooped and gathered up Mary's clothing. 'Do exactly as I say!' he demanded curtly, crouching at the edge of the water and reaching out, thrusting the clothes towards his wife. Her eyes were wide with fear as she listened to him. 'Go along this side of the lake until you find some thick brush. Don't make any noise. Get dressed, but don't come back here until I tell you.'

'But, Jubal —'

'Hurry, honey,' he pleaded. 'Do it!'

The concern in his voice and in his face forced Mary to do as he instructed, taking the bundle of clothes from him and beginning to wade along the edge of the lake. As Jubal rose, turned and moved towards the wagon, the lake bed shelved away and Mary suppressed a yell of alarm. She kicked up her legs and pushed the clothes out in front of her, propelling herself silently out of sight around the outward arc of a curve of bank.

Just as Jubal reached into the wagon and jerked out the Spencer, working the action to lever a shell into the breech, four riders crested the rise at a gallop. They saw him immediately and slowed their mounts to a walk on the downward incline.

The massive Luke Travers rode at one end of the line. The other men were all big and beefy by normal standards, but seemed almost stocky alongside the giant enforcer.

'Howdy, mister,' Travers greeted with an amiable grin as he moved slightly ahead of the others to lead them into the gap between the trees.

Jubal responded with a nod, aiming the Spencer negligently at the ground, but tensed to jerk it aloft at the first sign of danger.

'Saw the glint of water through the trees and got the same idea you had, I guess. Fine camping place, yes indeed.'

He halted his horse six feet away from where Jubal was standing at the front of the wagon, and the other men jerked on their own reins.

'Just getting ready to move out,' Jubal said. 'You can have the spot to yourselves.'

Travers swung out of the saddle and, taking their actions from the big man, the other three did likewise a moment later. Unlike Travers, who was dressed in an expensive city suit, the trio wore denim pants and check shirts. They might have been farmers except for their gun-belts with tied-down holsters fitted with Colt six-shooters. All four wore low-crowned, wide brimmed hats ideal for a long day's riding under a hot sun.

'Like for you to stay awhile, mister,' Travers countered brightly.

Jubal became more tense. The three smaller men were trying to appear as friendly as Travers, but the strain was showing in their sweat-run faces. They couldn't hold Jubal's steady gaze and kept dropping their eyes to glance at the Spencer. 'Particular reason?'

'Talk,' Travers said.

'About what?'

Travers kept the smile steadily in place, but his tone suddenly held a timbre of the ominous. 'Oh, wagons. I got a particular interest in wagons, mister. Probable you heard a shot back there on the road. My buddies here were riding on ahead of me and then I saw where a wagon rolled off the side and headed over here. Just had to come take a look. Fired a shot to get my buddies back with me from down the road.'

The big man was scatching the left side of his chest with his right hand. Suddenly it darted out of sight under his jacket lapel. A split second later, the hand re-appeared, balled into a fist and clutched around the butt of a double-action Starr .44.

'With this here gun, matter of fact,' the big man continued, pointing the revolver at Jubal. 'Bat an eyelid and you'll hear another shot.'

Jubal had seen the bulge of the shoulder holster under the big man's jacket, but been caught out by Travers' incredible speed of draw. He thought he could level the Spencer and get off at least one shot before the Starr blasted death at him. But what was the use? He let go of the rifle and it dropped almost silently on to the grass.

'What do you really want?' he asked.

'Told you,' Travers replied, waving the revolver to indicate that Jubal should move to the side. 'Talk about wagons. Where'd you get this one?'

Jubal side-stepped several paces and glanced into the trees fringing the area of lake shore where Mary was hidden. There was no sign of her. 'Dealer on 17th Street in New York,' he answered.

Travers nodded as he moved in close to the wagon and ran his fingertips over the smooth wood at the side where a name had been rubbed off. As he slid the Starr back into his shoulder holster, two of the smaller men drew their Colts. The third picked up the Spencer and examined it admiringly.

'Wagon was stolen.'

'Police?' Jubal asked.

The two men covering him laughed.

'No,' Travers answered, swinging away from the wagon to stare hard at Jubal. 'Work for the man the wagon was stolen from. Pretty big man in New York. Biggest. He gets to stay that way by not allowing anybody to screw him up. If just one guy got away with stealing from him, every deadbeat in the

East might chance his luck.'

The sweat of fear oozed from Jubal's pores, to trickle down over the tackiness which the heat had previously squeezed over his flesh. 'He's got to have it back, uh?'

'Right,' Travers agreed. 'So you'll need to buy another. But you won't get it from Reed the Weed.'

Jubal licked beads of saline moisture from his top lip. 'Not in business anymore?'

The personable grin appeared on the round face again. 'Let's just say we made New York a little hot for the Weed. Just stay where you are, mister.'

Travers approached Jubal from the side, taking care not to step in front of the two Colts pointed at the helpless man. His gait was casual, but as he neared Jubal, he displayed his speed again. He halted abruptly, thrust out an arm and curled his hand around Jubal's wrist. His fingers clenched tight and he jerked. Jubal was whipped in towards the big man, his stomach crashing hard into a thrust-out hip. The wind rushed out of Jubal's lungs and the trees at the side of the clearing were suddenly blurred as he was whirled around. Travers' free hand fastened upon Jubal's free wrist and jerked. Jubal was halted abruptly, balls of pain exploding in his shoulders as both his arms were trapped in a double hammer lock at his back. When he shook his head, clearing his vision, he saw the Colts sliding back into holsters as the two men approached him. In the background, the other man was levelling the Spencer in a token threat.

'Now you had no way of knowing where the wagon came from, mister,' Travers said softly, so close to his ear that Jubal could feel the big man's hot breath bending the short hairs on the back of his neck. 'So you get to stay alive. But your timing was wrong. You hadn't got to the Weed before me, we'd have been spared this long hot ride. So you've got to pay somehow, mister.'

The man on Jubal's left had a harelip. He threw the first punch – a telegraphed roundhouse that crashed powerfully into the area just above Jubal's heart. Jubal screwed his eyes tight shut and clamped his teeth hard together, fighting not to

38

release a sound of his pain.

'So we'll just rough you up a bit,' Travers muttered in his ear. 'Then Boss Egan'll be happy to have his wagon back and we won't feel so bad about having to ride all the way out here.'

The second man started his punch from a crouch, angling his fist straight to the centre of Jubal's stomach. His mouth was ripped open by the rush of escaping air and Travers allowed him to fold forward. The man with the harelip stepped in close and powered up his knee. The cap caught Jubal solidly under the jaw, flinging his body upright. Jubal's teeth crunched together and he tasted the grit of shattered enamel in his mouth. He spat and a moan of pain gained an involuntary exit. As a hand began to slap him, palm and knuckles landing stinging blows on his cheeks, rocking his head back and forth, he tried to find the reason why it was important not to make a noise.

'Pity it's happening to you,' Travers said softly into his ear, his breath seeming hotter than before. 'Innocent party. But that's life, ain't it? Win a little, lose a little.'

Mary! He had the reason. A knee crashed into his crotch and he didn't know whether or not he screamed. The roaring in his ears – like the big man's breath had become a hot, raging wind – drowned out all other sound. He hoped he was keeping silent. Perhaps Mary could not see into the clearing. If she could not, the sounds of the beating might be even more frightening.

Travers no longer allowed Jubal to ride with the blows. The man with the Spencer realized that if there ever had been a need to keep Jubal covered it had certainly passed now. The helpless man was still conscious for a low groan erupted from his slack mouth as each blow landed. But he was utterly limp in the grip of the massive Travers, all his weight supported by his tortured shoulders as his arms were folded up his back in the double hammer locks.

The two men engaged in delivering the beating had ceased to land alternate blows. Now, one stood back to allow his partner to throw punches at Jubal's head and body: then stepped forward to continue when the first was tired.

Gradually, as Jubal reached that far edge of pain where the body can accept more punishment but the nerve ends can suffer no greater degree of agony, his face was pummeled into a discoloured parody of human features. Both his eyes were closed by purple and blue bruises; his nose was a squashed, scarlet pulp and his lower lip was split almost from end to end. A dozen cuts and burst swellings marked his forehead, cheeks and jaw and each clenched first that smacked against his tortured flesh exloded a shower of blood drops.

'Enough!' Travers barked finally, as the man with the hare-lip backed away and the other man with blood-stained fists moved forward. He released his hold and Jubal crumpled, his legs folding like India rubber and his body collapsing to the side, useless arms unable to break the fall so that his head smacked into the grass-covered ground. It was, to Jubal, like falling on to a feather bed, but this final impact was sufficient to drive his mind into unconsciousness. 'I reckon he's got the message about the trouble he caused us.'

The other three laughed.

Among the trees, Mary stayed pressed to the soft covering of long-fallen leaves, paralysed with fear. She had heard every sound from the clearing by the lakeside: had desperately wanted to crash clear of the trees and plead for Jubal. But her husband's command to stay out of sight was imprinted in her mind and fear was not all-engulfing. Part of her mind was able to reason that there was nothing she could do. Her time would come when, mercifully, the men rode off and left Jubal.

'Lot of stuff inside, Luke,' one of the men announced. 'Looks like he was fixing for a long trip.'

'Let's have a look see!' the man with the harelip shouted excitedly.

As the man made to run towards the wagon, Travers shot out a meaty hand and clamped it around his arm, jerking him to a halt. 'Boss Egan don't pay you enough, Ryan?' he asked with soft menace.

Ryan gulped. 'Sure, Luke. But Boss ain't gonna want the little runt's stuff.'

'Boss said fetch back the wagon, is all,' Travers said, glanc-

40

ing from Ryan to the others. 'He ain't no small time sneak thief. Toss the guy's gear out and hitch a couple of our own nags to the wagon. We ain't taking nothing don't belong to Boss.'

'Hell, he ain't gonna need any of it!' the man in the rear of the wagon croaked, nodding towards the inert, raggedly breathing Jubal. 'He'll be dead before dinner time.'

'You wanna be there to welcome him?' Travers asked softly, releasing Ryan and jerking the man's Colt from the tied-down holster.

'Jesus, Luke!' the man in the wagon whined. 'Don't get snotty. Just an idea.'

'A lousy one,' Travers muttered. 'If ever I need one, I'll ask somebody else. Toss the stuff out.'

The Cades' trunks, valises and supplies were hurled roughly from the rear of the wagon while the other two men unsaddled two of their horses and hitched them. The other two saddle horses were tied to the tailgate and all four men climbed aboard the wagon, Travers taking the reins.

Ryan sat at the rear, eyeing the inert form of Jubal lying in an untidy heap on a patch of grass stained red with his own blood. 'Remind me never to cross up Boss Egan,' he said with disgust, and spat as the wagon jerked forward.

'And that guy didn't even know what he was doing,' another man muttered.

'Tough world,' Travers growled from the seat.

'Reckon the runt'll be glad to get out of it,' Ryan replied sourly as the wagon rolled over the crest of the rise and headed for the road.

CHAPTER FIVE

Prickly brush snagged at Mary's sodden dress as she fought her way through the trees. Beaded tears mingled with the perspiration on her face as she burst into the clearing for she was certain Jubal was dead. His face was coated with a shiny redness and his clothes and the grass around him picked up the colour. Although the wagon was out of sight, she could still hear the rumble of its wheels and she had an impulse to snatch up the discarded Spencer and stagger in pursuit. In that instant, the most important thing in her world was to see Jubal's torturers tumble into their own spurting blood as she poured hot lead into their evil bodies.

But then the futility of such a hate-inspired gesture struck forcefully home to her. She got as far as stooping to pick up the Spencer: and stopped. Mary had never in her life touched a gun and her natural revulsion for firearms rose nausea to her throat as her fingertips came within inches of brushing the rifle stock.

For long moments, she was frozen into immobility by a fear as strong as that which had held her a prisoner among the trees. The wagon at last rolled out of earshot and the whole world was a dead, silent place growing hotter by the moment and threatening to pitch her into senselessness.

Jubal groaned.

Birds sang and the water of the lake lapped the shore. The nausea sank from the brink of eruption and the tide of unconsciousness receded. Mary whirled and threw herself down beside her husband. She hugged his blood-dripping head to her breast and a gasp of elation ripped from her as she saw his chest rise and fall.

'Jubal!' she whispered.

His lips moved. Blood bubbled at the nostrils of his pulped

nose. Two tiny strips glinted beneath the discoloured puffiness of his eyebrows.

'They gone, honey?' he asked in a pained whisper, the words surfacing through bubbling moisture in his throat.

'Yes, darling,' Mary replied, quelling an involuntary urge to laugh. But a moment later pity for his terrible injuries threatened tears. She fought against these, too. 'What can I do, Jubal? Please tell me, darling.'

'Shade,' he croaked. 'Then hot water. Bandages.'

It was a slow, painful process to ease Jubal out of the heat of the afternoon sun and into the dappled shade of the trees. He weighed heavier than his compactness appeared and although he was fully conscious there was not an iota of strength in his body. Mary was terrified of adding to his pain. But at last he was out of the direct heat of the blazing sun, his bloodied head resting on his folded jacket.

At first, delayed shock hindered Mary as she built and lit a fire, then filled every pot with lake water and set them among the flames. It came in the form of violent trembling which attacked every muscle in her body and demanded release in the screams of free-reined hysteria. But somehow, she detached herself from the need, steeling herself to be concerned only with Jubal's plight and ignoring her own.

She talked to herself continuously, as if her mind had lost the ability to transmit coherently to her body and needed the medium of the voice. It worked, as she rifled her trunk, tearing her clothing into strips for bandages, then searching Jubal's valise of medical supplies for salving ointment.

While Mary was making these preparations, Jubal hovered on the edge of unconsciousness, sometimes aware of the green-tinted sunlight filtered through the trees and at others cloaked in pitch darkness. In this state, pain was nothing more than a dull ache concentrated nowhere in particular.

But then his wife began to bathe his face. The water revived him and added bite to his agony. He felt as though he were on fire from his stomach to the top of his head. Mary tended him with supreme gentleness, her expression of horror deepening as she wiped away the blood to reveal the ugly bruising and

43

countless wounds that made her husband's face almost un-recognizable.

Then, when the bleeding was stopped and she had coated the areas of broken skin with salve, she carefully stripped him to the waist. He had a little strength back by this time and was able to offer feeble help, groaning at each small movement.

'Is anything broken, Jubal?' Mary asked anxiously as she saw the almost complete area of blackened skin that extended from his lower stomach to his throat.

She had to lift his hands on to his own body and then waited, fighting another paroxysm of shivering, as his experienced fingers explored his flesh.

'Feels like every rib's gone, honey,' he rasped. 'But that's just inside. Have to wait and see, I guess. Bind me up, tight as you can make it.'

This was the most painful process of all. He had to hold himself in a sitting position while Mary used yard after yard of makeshift bandage to encase him in a constricting dressing. When it was finished and he could stretch out flat again, it took a long time for the pain to subside. Then he slept – too soon. He wanted to talk to Mary: tell her he was going to be all right and she should sit tight and wait. But the sleep hit him with the suddenness of unconsciousness. But it was sleep – his breathing easy and regular. Mary looked at him for a long time before deciding this. Then she allowed the shock to overtake her. First she took blankets from the bedroll, wrapped herself in them and lay down close to Jubal. The sun was as hard and harsh as it had ever been in the sky. But the blueness of its background was suddenly ice cold and it was this which attacked her: penetrating the blanket, freezing her sodden dress and chilling her trembling flesh clean through to the bones. She kept her teeth clenched tightly together, but soon she was unable to stop them chattering. The noise they made resounded inside her skull. Then her mouth gaped wide and she began to scream – louder and louder until her throat became dry: blocking exit to further sound.

Jubal slept through it all and soon a different kind of exhaustion overcame Mary, enfolding her into a deep, refreshing, natural sleep.

Pain triggered Jubal into a fast awakening and for long moments he stared into the darkness and tried to prod his memory into recall. Events zoomed in out of the past in chronological order and as his memory offered up images of the four horsemen riding into the clearing, fear for Mary's safety gripped him. But then the entire incident, interrupted by his unconsciousness, was unfurled.

He sat up. Fire raged in his chest, but not hot enough to signify broken bones. He was not blind. It was night, heavy with cloud. But the embers of the fire Mary lit still glowed dully and enabled him to see her face above the blankets. The blankets moved regularly with her rhythmic breathing. His face formed a smile, activating smarting pains in his cheeks, jaw and lips. A sound caused him to turn quickly, painfully. The two horses regarded him vacantly and he broadened the smile. He was alive and so was Mary. That was all that mattered.

His legs were weak but uninjured. His arms hurt from shoulders to elbows, but his hands were in good shape. He got slowly to his feet and moved around carefully, testing himself. He felt as if the slightest breeze would knock him down again but the pain did not reach the kind of pitch which a serious internal injury would signal.

The fact that his attackers had left the horses and contents of the wagon surprised him but he didn't waste time considering their possible motive. He built up the fire, filled two pots from the lake and started a beef stew and some coffee.

'Jubal! You shouldn't be doing that!'

The cool night air at the lake side was permeated with the delicious odours of boiling coffee and simmering stew. Jubal's bruised face, smeared with white ointment, looked ghastly in the flickering firelight. When he grinned at her, she saw that two of his teeth were broken.

'Maid's night off,' he said, his voice much stronger than the last time she had heard it.

She untangled herself from the blanket and shivered – but from the cold rather than shock. The fire felt as good as the

45

bubbling pots smelled.

'How do you feel, darling?' she asked anxiously as she crouched down beside him, wanting to put her arms around him but afraid of hurting him.

'As if one guy held me while two others used me for a punching bag,' he said, holding the grin in place. 'But it seems I had a good second.'

'I'll get the plates.' Mary said, after looking at him carefully for a long time, assuring herself that his lightness was not some strange side effect of the beating.

She ladled out the stew and they ate in silence, both suddenly ravenously hungry. Not until they were drinking the strong coffee did Mary break the long pause.

'Why did they do it, Jubal?'

'Wagon didn't belong to the guy I bought it from,' he answered. 'Seems the guy he stole it from was angry to lose it.'

'Men would go to this extreme to —'

'I took a chance, honey,' Jubal cut in. 'At the price I paid for the rig, I knew it had to be a crooked deal.' He grinned. 'But I didn't reckon on anybody being quite so upset about it.'

'Oh, Jubal,' Mary chided. 'Surely we could have stayed somewhere less expensive and you could have bought a wagon honestly?'

He put down his empty mug and clasped her hand. 'Make me a promise, honey?'

'What's that, Jubal?'

'Next time you think I'm going about something the wrong way, tell me?'

'I didn't know what you were doing in New York,' she pointed out.

Jubal nodded and squeezed her hand. 'You'll have to make allowances for the odd mistake, honey. It's the first time I've been married. I've got to get used to sharing my plans.'

Mary nodded and smiled, then looked around her helplessly – at the horses without a wagon to pull or saddles to wear and the scattering of baggage and supplies tossed across the clearing. 'What do we do now?'

'Sleep first, I reckon,' Jubal replied. 'I still feel as weak as a day old baby. And anyway, things never seem quite so bad after sun up.'

'They certainly can't look any worse,' Mary said with a sigh.

'Hey!' Jubal rebuked, releasing her hand and chucking her under the chin. 'You're the one who's supposed to look on the bright side of things.'

Mary forced a thin smile as she brushed a wave of hair out of her eyes. Her lips parted to say something, but clamped together again. Her face became a stiff mask of fear.

'Quick!' Jubal hissed, catching hold of her hand again and getting to his feet.

The wagon was out on the turnpike, being hauled at a slow pace. By the time the rumble of its turning wheels and the weary clop of the team's hooves were muffled as it left the hard-packed road for grass, Jubal and Mary were crouched behind the bulk of the two trunks. Jubal had the Spencer in his hands, resting across the top of one of the trunks. There was already a bullet in the breech.

'Please not again,' Mary whispered.

'Bright side, honey,' Jubal urged, but kept his eyes riveted on the crest of the rise.

In less than a minute, the smooth line of the hill top was broken by the silhouette of a covered wagon hauled by a two horse team, with a saddle horse tied on at the rear. There were two people up on the high seat, more dark shapes against the darker canvas.

'Whooooaaa,' the driver drawled, hauling on his reins. The wagon rumbled to a halt. There was a low mumble of conversation. Then: 'Anyone down there?'

'One's a woman, Jubal,' Mary hissed softly.

Jubal nodded without glancing at his wife. 'Somebody,' he called. 'With a rifle aimed right at your heart, mister.'

The woman on the wagon gasped.

'Okay,' the man called nervously. 'We'll be on our way. Didn't mean to disturb nobody. Me and the wife and kids just looking for a good place to rest up the night.'

His hand moved towards the brake.

'It's wrong to scare them off, Jubal,' Mary urged, with a

47

hint of the tentative.

He showed his broken teeth grin then stood up, holding the rifle but allowing it to point at the trunks. He knew he was clearly silhouetted against the light background of the lake.

'Come on down,' he called.

There was another murmuring of low voiced conversation, but it halted abruptly when Mary straightened from behind the trunks. The appearance of a woman re-assured the couple on the wagon. The reins were flicked across the backs of the team and the brake was released. The wagon rolled into the gap between the trees.

'Dana Prescott,' the driver said as he jumped down, then reached up to help the woman. 'This here's my wife, Lorna.'

The couple were in their early forties. Prescott was a big, broad-shouldered man with short-cropped red hair above a rugged, work weary face heavily lined by time and weather. He had a New England accent. His wife was almost as tall as he, but very thin. Her face also showed traces of a bitter struggle with life but these could not quite mask the basically beautiful structure of her features.

'Jubal Cade and Mary Cade,' Jubal introduced, taking the big man's hand and nodding to Lorna Prescott.

'You had some trouble here?' the man asked.

Jubal grinned. 'Some.'

'It accounts for our rather unfriendly greeting,' Mary explained. 'Our wagon was stolen by some men who were not content to leave it at that. I'll make some more stew.'

Lorna Prescott looked from Jubal to Mary and back again, recognizing that while the man bore the scars, he was not the only one to be suffering. 'That you will not,' she countered. 'You both seem ready to drop where you stand. So you get some rest.'

'Mommy, I'm hungry.'

'You be patient, Andy.'

Both voices came from within the wagon. The first was that of a young boy: the second, a girl, older.

'The kids,' Prescott explained. 'Andy and Chrissy.'

'We can make the introductions come morning,' his wife

urged, with a kindly smile. 'You two bed down now.'

The alarm caused by the arrival of the Prescotts' wagon had drained both Jubal and Mary of a large amount of the energy which the stew and coffee had restored to them. They needed no further encouragement from the tall, thin woman and her rather confused husband to follow Lorna's suggestion.

'Where you folks headed?' Jubal asked as he stretched out beneath his blankets and closed his eyes, listening to the subdued sounds of the Prescotts preparing their supper.

'California at the end,' Dana answered. 'First off to Independence.'

'Long time until dawn, but it's looking better already, honey,' Jubal whispered to Mary.

Her hand reached out over the strip of grass separating them and her fingers interlocked with his. She squeezed gently.

'You reckon they're brother and sister, Lorna?' Dana Prescott said softly as he lifted a box of supplies from the rear of the wagon. 'They didn't say.'

Lorna looked across the clearing and on the very fringe of the firelight she saw the clasped hands. 'Don't reckon so, Dana,' she whispered with a smile, and moved smoothly into the routine of preparing a meal for her hungry family.

CHAPTER SIX

Prescott roused his wife and children an hour before dawn with mugs of hot, strong coffee and plates of salt bacon and beans. He had prepared enough to feed the Cades as well, but was reluctant to wake them. So it was left to Lorna to shake Mary's shoulder and she roused Jubal.

The edge of pain had been dulled and a stiffness in his muscles was his main enemy. His face looked worse than ever for there was hardly one part of it that had not taken on a dull but nevertheless angry coloration. And the sprouting of twenty-four hours of bristle which he could obviously not shave off added to his rather grotesque appearance.

Young Andrew Prescott even ran to his mother's side and clutched her skirts when he saw Jubal sit up and firelight fell across the bruised and lacerated features.

'I'm not as bad as I look, son,' Jubal said, showing his broken-toothed grin.

'You sure look bad,' the boy said, shaking his head.

He was ten years old, lithe and strong-looking for his age, with a mop of unruly blond hair above a snub-nosed, wide-eyed face that owed more to his mother's former beauty than his father's rugged features.

His sister was in her mid-teens with a slim build beginning to fill out towards womanhood. She would not be as beautiful as Andy would be handsome, but she had a pleasant, finely sculptured face framed by shoulder length blonde hair that had a healthy sheen in the firelight.

'Kinda family tradition that I make breakfast,' Prescott said, a trifle embarrassed. 'Ain't good, but it's filling.'

He was right on both counts, but Jubal and Mary acted the polite guests and offered fulsome praise as they washed down the greasy food with bitter coffee. They boy was fascinated by

Jubal's injuries and stared at him, open-mouthed, as he related what had happened by the lakeside yesterday afternoon.

'Gee, I bet it must have hurt!' the boy exclaimed.

Jubal grinned, 'In the pride, most of all.'

'Three against one – that ain't fair!' the boy protested.

'Isn't,' his mother corrected.

Andy shrugged, and at last began to eat his breakfast as his father offered the family's story in exchange for Jubal's. He had been a tenant farmer in Maine with no hope of ever owning his own land there. They would have gone West a long time ago, but Andy's birth had held them back and they had resolved to pull up stakes the day the boy reached the age of ten. Prescott's decision to forsake the newly linked Central and Union Pacific trans-continental railroad was the same as Jubal's – he wanted to see the country with a greater freedom than a passenger car would allow.

After the meal, when Lorna had washed the dishes and the Cades were at the lake side, Mary bathing Jubal's face and applying fresh salve to the angriest looking scars, Dana Prescott approached them with the familiar embarrassed look on his careworn face.

'We ain't ... haven't come out and asked you, Mr. and Mrs. Cade,' he began haltingly. 'But I reckon you might have figured it ... We'd – Lorna and me and the kids – be happy to have you join us since you lost your wagon. Be kinda crowded in my rig, but if you don't mind that, we sure don't. Glad of the company.'

'That would be wonderful, Mr. Prescott!' Mary exclaimed.

'One condition,' Jubal said earnestly.

Both looked at him anxiously. 'You call us Mary and Jubal,' he said, the grin spreading across his battered face.

Prescott smiled shyly. 'That works both ways, Jubal.'

'Mister's wrong anyway,' Mary pointed out. 'Jubal's a doctor.'

Jubal had to maintain his grin while Prescott gave him a long look. 'Well, how about that,' the farmer said in delight.

When he went to help his wife pack away the breakfast things, Jubal sighed.

'What's wrong?' Mary asked.

'Do me a favour, honey,' he said ruefully. 'Don't tell too many people I'm a doctor unless there's real need. Some folks only need to know there's a medical man around and they suddenly find a thousand and one things wrong with them.'

'Oh, you!' she said with a laugh. 'It's about time you did some work. All those years of learning how to be a doctor and you haven't even opened your medical bag since you got your M.D.'

'Physician heal thyself,' he said with another sigh, then smiled and stole a kiss while Mary checked the binding around his chest.

'I saw you, I saw you!' Andy chanted in delight, and managed to duck under a reprimanding swipe from his mother.

The sun was up and heading for the concealment of a damp-looking cloud bank when the wagon, heavier with two extra passengers and their baggage rolled out on to the turnpike. But the morning stayed fine. Mary and Lorna came to an arrangement about preparing alternate meals with the unfortunate rider that Dana was still to be allowed to use his questionable culinary talents each breakfast time. And, despite the older man's protests that Jubal should rest until he was fully fit, the chore of driving the wagon was divided equally.

The rain came in a deluge at mid-afternoon and kept up incessantly for the next three days and nights, turning the roads into quagmires and slowing progress to a struggling crawl. But across Pennsylvania and the northern tip of West Virginia the weather held good.

Inevitably, there were minor irritations between two such different families living at such close quarters, but the Cades and Prescotts both took great pains to subjugate visible reactions to these frictions. The Prescotts were not hypochondriacs and Jubal's medical skills were only called upon in genuine need – when Andy caught the whooping cough, Chrissy cut herself and the wound became infected and Dana sprained his ankle in a rabbit hole.

As the miles slipped by, so the signs of Jubal's beating disappeared until at length there were only the two broken teeth

– at top and bottom on the right side – and some unhealable scar tissue on the bridge of his nose to show that he had been so brutally attacked. The moustache – for some reason grey in colour – which he had failed to remove when he was able to shave again, could not really be counted as a remnant of the beating. He chose to keep it – bushy along his top lip and drooping a short way at each corner of his mouth – simply because he liked it. He would not reveal the real reason: that it robbed his features of their boyishness when he grinned.

Ohio and Indiana rolled under the wheels of the wagon as the journey ceased to be counted in days. And then the weeks grew into months. In central Illinois, with the St. Louis crossing of the Mississippi River the next major objective, Jubal's small reserve of money was finally exhausted. Just as the chores were divided equally between the adults, so were the expenses – for fresh supplies, repairs to the wagon and shoes for the two teams of horses. Jubal and Mary had discussed their lack of money in private as they collected kindling for the night camp's fire and Jubal announced their decision while Lorna and Mary were washing the dishes after the evening meal.

'We'll be leaving you in St. Louis,' he said as both men drew against cheroots, huddled close to the blazing fire which kept the chill bite of the fall air at bay.

On the far side of the fire, Andy and Chrissy snapped up their eyes from the books which each had to study every night before bedding down. The orange glow high-lighted the disappointment inscribed on their faces. Dana Prescott's expression was quizzical. Jubal could hear the murmur of low-voiced conversation over by the wagon and knew Mary was saying much the same thing to Lorna.

'I guess you got a reason?' Prescott asked, embarrassed again, for the first time since the meeting by the lake. He was a man who enjoyed routine and any unexpected turn of events plunged his mind into a turmoil of indecision. He was lucky to have such a capable wife.

'We're making this trip to see the country as well as to get where we're going,' Jubal reminded. 'Mary and I'd like to spend some time in the mid-West before heading on.'

'Go to bed, kids,' Prescott instructed.

'Aw!' Andy complained.

Chrissy, old enough to have the ability to sense when adult conversation was in the offing, grabbed her brother's arm and urged him towards the prepared bedrolls beneath the wagon, silencing his protests with urgent whispers.

'If that's the only reason you got, Lorna and me will be happy to know you're doing what you want, son,' Prescott said thoughtfully. 'But I saw how you had to scrape around in your pockets to rake up enough for the blacksmith back down the trail. So if it's money, I got more than enough to keep two extra fed and everything else is my responsibility anyway – since it's my wagon.'

Jubal tried to interrupt, but the older man held up a hand.

'Wouldn't be no loan, either. If we didn't have you along, we'd have had to pay doctor's bills, son.'

'Well, that's a fine attitude to —'

'Jubal!' Mary's voice, sharp with warning, cut across the campsite like a whipcrack, instantly silencing her husband.

Both men sensed the urgency of her interruption. But for long seconds the silence was disturbed only by the crackle of drying brush consumed by the flames. Then, as Jubal and Dana Prescott stood up, seeing the still, tense postures of their wives, they heard the hoofbeats.

The camp was set in a small hollow formed by grassy hillocks on three sides and a rocky escarpment on the other. A major reason for choosing the place to spend the night was a small stream which sprang from the foot of the forty foot high rock face and ran clear and slow for a hundred feet before boring underground again to tunnel through the base of a hill. Mixed timber cloaked the rise to the west while to east and north the slopes were spread with grass and low brush. The horsemen – at least half a dozen – were approaching from the north.

'The fire!' Lorna exclaimed.

'Too late,' her husband countered, striding towards the wagon with Jubal in his wake.

The moon was an inspired patch behind a veil of cloud. The

54

fire was large, its flickering light reflected by the white rock of the cliff face. All knew their position was marked by a soft orange glow in the night which could be seen for miles around.

Prescott passed the Spencer out of the wagon to Jubal, and scooped up his own almost new Winchester. 'Inside,' he instructed the children curtly, then turned. 'You, too.'

Jubal nodded as Mary looked at him anxiously and the women climbed up after the children.

Visitors to their camp were nothing new to the travellers. On a number of occasions their evening routines had been interrupted by other families heading west, or single riders bound in all directions. But never before had they been approached by a group of horesmen riding at a full gallop. The sound of the thundering hooves vibrating in the cool night air, swelling as the group drew closer, had a harsh, menacing quality. The five grazing horses picked up the tension from the humans and scraped at the ground, their ears pricked and nostrils flared.

'Let's get hid,' Prescott urged, backing away from the wagon and jerking his Winchester to indicate that Jubal should go in the opposite direction.

The wagon was parked at the foot of the escarpment, on the far side of the fire from the approaching riders. Prescott moved to the right and crouched behind a heap of boulders that had crashed from the cliff-face in some pre-historic rockfall. Jubal went to the right, into the cover of the trees sprouting on the slope of the western rise. He had to splash across the narrow, shallow stream to reach the timber.

As he listened to the rising volume of hoofbeats, he looked towards the wagon and saw the faces of the women and children as pale blobs against the darkened interior. Prescott had made what was probably one of the few fast decisions in his life and, Jubal felt with a stab of fear, it was the wrong one. It would have been better had everyone sought the cover of the timber. But he held off from framing mental criticism of the older man, aware that the nod of encouragement he had given Mary was his seal of approval on the hurried defensive plan. And why look for danger until it became apparent it was there to be seen?

Eight riders crested the rise and skidded their mounts to a snorting halt. The sight of them was ominous enough to cause Jubal to lever a shell into the Spencer's breech. In the sudden, short silence that followed the end of the gallop, he thought he heard the metallic scraping of the Winchester's action.

The newcomers held their position on the crest of the rise for only a few seconds, then the man at their head heeled his horse into a walk and the others, massed into a tight bunch, followed him. Against the skyline they were silhouettes, then they became a moving shadow on the dark rise, with the occasional glint of firelight dancing off guns and harness rings. At the edge of the fire's glow, they divided into a curved line and halted, showing themselves with a casual arrogance.

They were all in their twenties and early thirties, all tall, hard-faced, travel-stained and attired in shirts, levis, fur-lined jackets and plainsman hats in subdued colours. All wore gun-belts, three of them with a holster at each thigh. Rifle stocks poked up from boots behind their saddles. The horses' flanks were white with lather and the men's grizzled and dirt-streaked faces were sheened with the air-cooled sweat of a hard ride.

'Looks like the folks want a game of hide and seek, McCabe,' one of the men drawled.

All their eyes glittered as the men peered from one side of the campsite to the other.

'We don't have the time for no games,' a man at the centre of the arc of mounted men replied easily. 'Let's flush 'em out.'

The men weren't fast on the draw, or perhaps they intended their move as a bluff. Prescott sent a shot whining over the centre of the line before a single revolver was levelled. The horses moved restlessly at the sudden sound, but the riders calmed them easily. The hand-guns came up to cover the camp, but nobody answered Prescott's shot. There was just the dry clicks of the cocking action as the hammers were thumbed back and the cylinders revolved.

'What you fellers want here?' Prescott asked, his voice calm and unhurried.

The intruders at each side of the centre turned to look at

their obvious leader. It was on this man's heart that Jubal drew a bead.

'Water the nags and a bite to eat for ourselves,' the man answered in the same tone, but his gaze steady as he concentrated on the heap of boulders where he knew Prescott was hiding. 'Name's McCabe. These here are my boys. Guess you heard of the McCabe Boys?'

'Stranger in these parts,' Prescott called.

McCabe nodded sagely. 'Should have figured that, feller. Or else you wouldn't have took a shot at me and the boys. Mighty dangerous shooting at us. Folks as know us figure it better just to let us take what we want. Then nobody gets hurt. Leastways, sometimes nobody gets hurt.'

Some of the men laughed.

'If you turn around and ride out as fast as you rode in, none of you'll get hurt,' Prescott answered.

'Gonna count to five,' McCabe said as if he had not heard the threat. 'If you ain't in sight with your hands high, gonna start blasting. Eight against one ain't no chance at all.'

'Against two!' Jubal called easily.

Every man in the line had swung his revolver towards the boulders. The new voice, coming from a different direction, startled them. Eyes and gun barrels swung towards the trees. McCabe recovered first.

'How many more?'

'Start shooting and find out,' Prescott taunted, a note of triumph in his voice as he saw the effect of Jubal's announcement.

Pondering the new situation, McCabe showed his thought processes on his face. He was in turn afraid, worried and undecided. Then, as somebody changed position in the wagon and caused it to creak on its springs, he returned to being confident.

'If both guys don't do like I said, blast the wagon, boys,' he instructed. 'Onetwofive.'

It wasn't a new trick to run the count together and miss out two numbers. Even as McCabe opened his mouth to start the count, he and the others were moving – huddling their bodies into a crouch and sliding fluidly from their saddles. The first shots were fired before their feet touched ground, aimed across the necks of the horses as the animals were jerked sideways-on for cover.

Eight ·45 calibre bullets ripped through the canvas covering of the wagon and three of them burrowed deep into Chrissy Prescott's head. It was her mother who screamed, as a great splash of blood and spattering of torn flesh lashed across her. She went on screaming, hugging the still warm but very dead body of her daughter to her.

Jubal Cade had no way of knowing who had been hit or who was screaming. He put the futility of guesswork into its proper place and concentrated his mind and physical reflexes on the obvious. The only clear targets he had were the legs of men among those of the horses and he aimed low. He fired three times, jerking the rifle to the right after each shot. Then he swung back along the line, pumping the action and squeezing the trigger three more times. Thus three men died, first collapsing in agony as their kneecaps were shattered, then taking bullets in the head to spray more blood beneath the stamping feet of their panicked horses.

Prescott – less of a crack shot – used a different tactic. He pumped ·44 calibre shells into the snorting animals and sent follow-up bullets towards the exposed men as their horses collapsed. He was not so fast or accurate as Jubal, but his Winchester had a twelve-shot magazine to the Spencer's seven-shot.

Horses, their reins swinging free of dead fingers, reared and bucked, ears pricked to the roar of gun-fire and nostrils flared to be filled by the stench of burnt powder. Winchesters, Spencers and a Le Mat were snatched from saddle boots and high velocity rifle fire poured into the wagon and towards the positions of the two defenders. Lorna Prescott cried her husband's name as a bullet drilled a hole through the centre of her hand. A second bullet entered the side of her throat and exited amid a gout of thick scarlet from her punctured jugular vein.

'Mommy!' Andy screamed, leaping to his feet.

Her body wracked with sobs, Mary hurled herself across the wagon and slammed her shoulder into the boy's legs. He went over backwards as a fusillade of shots thundered in the hollow. A bullet ricochetted off the bottom of a hanging pan, lost speed and lodged in the shattered bone just above Andy's nose. Mary threw herself on top of the boy and held him in a tight embrace as another shower of bullets whined through the tattered canvas and splintered rock from the face of the cliff.

The sound of his son's voice, ringing with terror, drove Prescott into an insane forward rush. He had no idea how many shells were left in the Winchester as he sprang up and leapt over the boulders, firing from the hip as he landed and ran. He killed two horses and one man before the final shellcase was ejected and the pin clicked into the void of an empty breech.

That tiny, awful sound was an isolated grotesque prick against a capsule of silence which had descended over the hollow. Prescott stopped abruptly and stared down hopelessly at his empty rifle. McCabe and three more survivors moved from behind their horses, faces split by broad grins. The gun fight had lasted less than a minute and for half that time there had been no shots from the trees. The quartet were sure the man in the timber was dead.

'You did good, but numbers beat you, feller,' McCabe rasped. Then he died.

Jubal exploded his final bullet towards a clear target. He fired from a crouch and the slug took McCabe under the chin and angled upwards, drilling a hole through his tongue and burrowing through the roof of his mouth into his brain. He was flipped over backwards, a fountain of blood issuing from his gaping lips and scattering into a myriad drops to fall like red rain.

But the other three were already squeezing their triggers and their rifles cracked as if in a single shot. Prescott's chest erupted scarlet blossoms in three places but even before his lifeless body smacked against the ground, his shirt front showed just one enormous stain.

As the three rifles were swung towards his position, Jubal

clawed out the tiny under-and-over Remington and pulled one trigger. The shot furrowed a bloody trail across the forehead of the man at the centre of the trio. He staggered, but stayed on his feet. Then:

'Let's get!' he yelled, flinging himself up into the saddle and thudding his heels into the sides of his horse.

Jubal let go the second shot from the tiny gun and it went wide. But it convinced the other two men to follow the shouted advice. They smacked the barrels of their rifles against the hindquarters of their horses and held on to the saddlehorns, hauling themselves clear of the ground from a run.

While they were still only halfway up the rise, Jubal broke from cover and splashed through the stream to run to the wagon. In the firelight he could see a steady drip of blood forming a pool beneath from a crack in the wagon bed. He heard a woman crying.

There was a flurry of movement and a shape loomed up in the flickering firelight that lapped through the many holes in the canvas top. Jubal recognized Mary, her features twisted into an ugly mask of terror. One arm was clutched around the limp body of Andy, pressing the boy close against her body. In the other hand she gripped the handle of a carving knife, ready to plunge the blade towards an attacker.

'It's me, honey,' Jubal said softly, then prepared to lunge to the side as he realized Mary's terrified mind did not accept her husband. For many seconds, he was just a man with a gun and it was men such as he who had rained flesh-exploding death around her.

Then he saw the glitter of tears in her eyes and the trembling of her lips and he knew she was coming out of mind-bending shock on to a different level.

'Jubal,' she whispered. She allowed the knife to slip from her fingers and looked down into the blood-run face of the boy. 'He's still breathing.'

Jubal gripped the top of the tailgate to haul himself into the wagon. But then he froze, listening. Mary's body became rock still with tension again. More hoofbeats drummed against the night's silence.

'Not again!' Mary exclaimed hoarsely, her eyes squeezing tears onto her cheeks as they screwed shut.

Jubal snatched up a carton of shells and dropped to the ground.

CHAPTER SEVEN

There were a dozen riders in the new group and they showed as many signs of a hard ride as McCabe and his men. But it was shock rather than curiosity which showed on their sweat-sheened faces as they drew their mounts to a halt at the top of the rise.

'Jesus Christ Almighty!' one of the men muttered in awe.

'He's from another place,' an older man at his side rasped. 'That down there looks like Hell.'

Their voices were very loud against the deathly hush which had dropped over the hollow immediately the hoofbeats ceased to thunder. For even the fire had ended its crackling, as if in deference to the dead. The bodies of McCabe and four of his men were sprawled among the carcases of their horses on one side of the fire, the blood of humans and animals merging to be soaked into the grassy ground. Beyond, Dana Prescott was spread-eagled, the fresh blood on his shirt front shining brighter than his dead, staring eyes. The bullet-scarred wagon kept its corpses concealed but seemed somehow to emanate an evil aura to hint at its grisly contents. Two of the travellers' horses grew stiff on their sides. The other three grazed peacefully as if in some quiet meadow.

'What you figure, sheriff?' somebody asked as the horses caught the scent of blood and stamped nervously. 'Looks like everybody's dead.'

A man of middle years with a drooping moustache and long sideburns tipped his hat on to the back of his head and raked his glittering eyes across the scene of carnage once more. 'Down there maybe,' he allowed. 'But McCabe had seven men and there ain't that many stiffs.'

He moved in his saddle and his coat fell open. The star on his chest caught the firelight.

'Three got away,' Jubal called, stepping out from the tree line.

Twelve pairs of suddenly nervous eyes swung to look at him and twelve hands dropped to grip revolver butts. But nobody drew. The small man standing on the bank of the stream was holding a rifle, but it was pointed at the ground. He was looking at the sheriff impassively and there was no hint of aggression in him.

'The McCabe Boys tried to rob you?' the lawman asked, heeling his horse forward. The others moved down the slope behind him.

'They tried,' Jubal replied, as Mary moved out into the open with Andy Prescott cradled in her arms.

The men looked at her with mild surprise, unmoved by the vivid blood on the boy's face and the woman's dress. They had seen so much of it already they were immune.

'Wasn't your money they wanted,' the sheriff said as he dismounted and looked at the face of each dead gunman in turn. 'Held up a bank a hundred miles north of here. Took close to fifty grand. We been pushing them hard. Reckon it was grub they was after.'

'Or maybe just hadn't killed anybody all day,' a voice put in sardonically.

'How many of you folks did they kill?' the lawman asked, jerking a thumb at the dead men and nodding to the members of the posse closest to the bodies.

'Boy's parents and sister,' Jubal answered.

The cadavers were wrapped in their own blankets and slung across the backs of horses. The sheriff stooped to examine the contents of the saddlebags on the dead animals. He found the one he wanted and cut it free. His lips, almost hidden by the moustache, cracked into a smile as he tested the weight.

'Feel like fifty thousand, sheriff?' a man asked.

'Ain't never had that much,' the lawman answered wryly. 'But it sure feels like a lot. And McCabe didn't have the time to share it out or spend any of it.'

'Jubal, they're going,' Mary said in a startled whisper as,

following the lead of the sheriff, the men remounted.

Jubal was as surprised as his wife. And for a moment amazement held him tongue-tied. Then: 'We've got a sick boy and dead to bury!' he called.

The posse was halted in the process of wheeling to head out of the hollow. The sheriff's expression of grim satisfaction was replaced by shallow sympathy.

'We're on official business, mister,' he said, his tone hard, his eyes glittering. 'Unless we get this money back to the bank real fast there's likely to be a riot.'

Jubal was suspicious of the motive. 'Those bodies will slow you down,' he pointed out.

Some of the men shifted uncomfortably in their saddles. Most were indifferent.

'Ain't none of your business, mister,' the lawman shot back, his tone even harsher. 'Be thankful we ain't leaving them for you to dig graves for.'

With this, he jerked on his reins to complete the turn and nudged his way through the group. He spurred his horse directly into a gallop and the rest of the posse went up the slope in his wake.

'My God, how can men be so . . . callous!' Mary hissed.

'Money,' Jubal answered, keeping his own anger low-keyed. He eased the unconscious boy from his wife's arms and splashed across the stream.

'They're stealing the bank money?' Mary asked incredulously.

'No,' Jubal told her. 'McCabe and his men must have had a price on their heads to keep the posse on their trail for so long. And the bodies will be needed to collect the rewards.'

Then both forgot about the brutal indifference of the posse to their plight as they heard the laboured breathing of the injured boy and looked at his blood-covered face.

'Jubal, he's going to die!' Mary exclaimed in a hushed whisper.

'Maybe not, honey,' he replied softly, and began to give her instructions.

Her husband's calmness, together with her own strength of

64

purpose to save Andy, allowed Mary to climb into the wagon and get what was required without the sight of the dead Lorna and Chrissy Prescott driving her into hysteria. She was like a cold machine, collecting unstained blankets, Jubal's medical bag, a pot to heat water and two kerosene lamps. Her emotions continued cold and her actions precise and mechanical as she helped Jubal prepare for what he had to do. Then, when everything was ready, she held the two lamps in rock-steady hands and found she was able to watch the operation without the least hint of squeamishness.

First, working with the utmost gentleness, Jubal swabbed off the blood from the immediate area of the wound in Andy's forehead. As the crust of congealed matter was removed, sluggish fresh blood oozed. But not before the deformed end of the ricochetted bullet could be seen. The surgeon's instruments, sterilized in boiling water, glinted in the firelight as Jubal probed, gripped the bullet and eased it out. He worked furiously, with the same light touch, to swab away the blood dotted with tiny bone fragments.

Mary desperately wanted to ask him if Andy had a chance, but bit her tongue to prevent herself from posing the question. For Jubal's face was a sweating mask of intense concentration and he did not relax until he had applied an antiseptic lotion and bound the boy's head. Then he straightened from his crouch over the prostrate form and mopped his face with his shirt sleeve. As he took the lamps from Mary, turned down the wicks to extinguish them and set them on the ground he could see the unasked question written in the set of her features.

'The frontal cranium is chipped but I can't tell whether it's cracked,' he told her. 'And there's no way of knowing whether there's brain damage or any vital nerves are affected.'

'But he's going to live?' Mary insisted.

Jubal looked down at the boy. His face was so pale his lips seemed to be a vivid red. His breathing was easier, but he was still unconscious rather than in a natural sleep. Sweat beaded his cheeks and jaw and was already discolouring the white dressing around his head.

'We have to wait, honey,' he said, stepping up to his wife

and looping an arm around her shoulders. When she turned her face to look at him, he gave her a reassuring smile. 'But I've got a feeling he'll pull through.'

Mary's nod was non-committal. She wanted to help Jubal bury the dead, but he told her it was important to keep a constant watch on the boy and make sure he stayed warm.

Clearing the campsite of the visible signs of death took the remainder of the night. First he buried the Prescotts, in separate but adjacent graves close to the bank of the stream. Then, using two of the surviving horses, he dragged the carcases deep into the timber and covered them with fallen and rotted leaves. It was easy to hide the bloodstains on the ground with fresh earth, but back-breaking to scrub them from the interior of the wagon.

Throughout the night, Mary kept the fire roaring fiercely and used a damp cloth to wipe the sweat from the pale face of the boy. Then, through the day, night, day, night and day that followed, the husband and wife took turns at attending to his simple but vitally important needs. No more visitors came to the hollow.

When Andy emerged from his coma and rasped weakly that he was hungry it was mid-afternoon. He thought it was night. He was blind.

CHAPTER EIGHT

It was three weeks before Jubal pronounced Andy Prescott well enough to travel. The little blond-headed boy, blessed with the natural resilience of the young, came through his ordeal with no other ill-effects apart from the blindness. And even this was not total, for he could differentiate between dark and light and see movement over short distances.

He would, Jubal felt sure, have recovered his physical strength sooner but his depression on hearing of the death of his parents and sister had a psychosomatic effect on him. But as time passed, and he experienced the love and care of Jubal and Mary, the boy came to accept them as more than adequate substitutes.

For their part, the Cades both sensed the kind of roles Andy had given them but if this aroused any concern within them, they did not voice it to each other. Their only spoken anxiety involved the need to get Andy to an eye doctor as soon as possible to discover whether there was a hope of restoring his sight to normal.

As the boy grew stronger each day and began to eat as well as he ever had, Mary could not understand Jubal's reluctance to leave the hollow with its haunting memories of wholesale slaughter. But Jubal was waiting for a sign, and it came early one morning when he and Andy were collecting fire kindling in the woods on the western slope. Jubal was telling the boy of how, during his early medical training in England, a mother had brought her young son to the hospital and demanded his stomach be cut open to retrieve a watch he had swallowed. The surgeon had sent the couple off with a large bottle of castor oil and the assurance that soon the time would pass away.

Of course, it was an old story and not true, but it made Andy laugh. Previously the boy had not even smiled and as his delight trilled through the timber Jubal decided it meant he was now ready to begin his new life. The wagon was hitched and they rolled out of the hollow immediately after breakfast.

Many small towns and settlements dotted the prairie of central Illinois. Few had a doctor of any sort and certainly none boasted a medical man with any more knowledge of Andy's affliction than Jubal. They considered swinging north towards Chicago, but that was further away than St. Louis so they held to their original destination.

Although it was full fall now the weather stayed dry and the sun shone on most days. Rain would have been a problem, for the patches of torn blanket with which Mary had repaired the canvas covering of the wagon were not waterproof. The terrain over which they travelled was for the most part flat and monotonous. The towns little more than clusters of farmhouses huddled together as if to combat loneliness from the vast expanses of wheatfields surrounding them, the soil fresh ploughed after the harvest.

At first, Andy's questions were widely spaced and hesitant. But gradually, as he came to realize that he was not an irritation, his thirst for information became more vocal. He rode up on the seat between Jubal and Mary and the couple found their eyes acting for him. Patiently, they explained the country around them and Andy listened in wrapt attention, ever-ready with supplementary questions.

'Another town up ahead,' Jubal told the boy as the far horizon showed up a group of buildings set on the rim between land and sky.

'Big one?' Andy asked, his young face expectant. Although the bullet had injured his optic nerve, his eyes seemed perfectly normally. They could move to left and right, up and down; and mirrored his emotions.

'Small,' Mary replied. 'It's still a long way off. There appears to be a river between the town and us. The farmland starts on the far side.'

'What's it like this side?'

Mary looked to left and right, across vast acres of tall grass featured here and there with a stand of leafless trees. She explained the scene to Andy, mentioning the colours and telling him how the grass moved like waves on the ocean as a gentle wind wafted at it from the north-west. Andy could feel for himself that, although the wind was slight, it had a keen edge. Since the dressing had been removed from his head, he was sensitive to temperature change and could even predict the weather ahead by the sensations he felt behind the small, circular white scar just above his nose.

'Very small, Andy,' Mary said. 'We don't have to ford this river. There's a wooden bridge. The road looks smoother on the other side. It goes between the buildings. Perhaps six on either side. All small houses, except for one, larger building. I can see a chicken in the street ... no, it's a small dog.'

Jubal had been staring at the town in thoughtful silence for a long time, trying to pinpoint what it was that aroused an indefinable foreboding within him. When he realized what it was, he interrupted Mary's description of the trestle bridge they were about to cross.

'... and the water is running very smoothly. It's deep because I can't see the bottom and ...'

'There's something strange about the town,' Jubal said in an ominous tone.

Mary shot an anxious glance towards her husband, saw the concern in his profile and swung her gaze back to the town.

'What is it?' Andy asked, his tone and expression worried as he sensed the mood of the adults.

The hooves of the team clattered on the wooden planking of the bridge and Mary put a comforting arm around the boy's narrow shoulders.

'There's nobody about,' Mary said, half thinking aloud and half satisfying the youngster's curiosity. 'But the best place is indoors on a day as cold as this.'

Jubal nodded, but his expression did not alter and he continued his close scrutiny of the buildings ahead. Mary's description had been accurate. There were about a dozen houses with a street running between them. They were all single storey. The larger building, which had two floors, housed both a saloon-hotel and a general store. As the wagon rolled between the first two houses, the small mongrel dog gave an aggressive bark. But then it yelped, put its tail between its legs and ran from sight behind a house.

'It's quiet,' Andy said, keeping his voice low.

It did not need finely attuned hearing, which was nature's compensation for lack of sight, to discern this aspect of the community's strangeness. But this was not the only sense which had become more fully developed since the boy's blindness.

'And I don't smell no smoke,' he augmented in the same hushed whisper.

'Any smoke,' Mary corrected automatically, matching the level of his voice.

Jubal nodded as he reined the horses to a halt and applied the brake in front of the two storey building. 'There is none, Andy,' he said in a normal tone and his voice seemed to echo between the façades of the buildings. 'It *is* cold and there ought to be a fire in the grate of every house.'

'A ghost town!' Andy said in awe, excited by the prospect.

Jubal stood up and looked both ways along the street. All the buildings were in a good state of repair with no broken panes in the windows. Some had been painted since last winter. Doors were firmly shut against the weather. A few of the houses had small gardens in front of them, neatly tended. The fields they had driven between showed every sign of having received careful attention after the harvest. But there was not a human soul to be seen – nor an animal since the dog had fled into hiding.

'Stay here!' Jubal instructed when he had completed his surveillance.

As he climbed down from the wagon, he slid the Spencer from behind the seat.

'He's taken his gun,' Andy whispered, and Mary tightened her embrace. She shivered – not entirely from the wind, which had suddenly increased in force and moaned forlornly as it drove through the gaps between the buildings.

Jubal levered a bullet into the breech as he went up the two steps and on to the stoop that stretched along the front of the saloon and store. Dust was lifted and eddied along in the path

70

of the wind. Although it was only mid-afternoon, the storm clouds gave the day a dusk-like quality. He smelt the nauseating odour of decomposed flesh even before the batswings folded away from him under the pressure of the rifle barrel.

There were four bodies, hanging from a thick beam which extended from one side of the saloon to the other. Their booted feet dangled some twelve inches from the sawdust covered floor. The two tables upon which they had stood awaiting execution rested on their sides behind the awfully still bodies. The men had been dead a long time, the rotting process beginning at the bullet wounds in their stomachs. They had been shot first, then strung up and had the tables kicked from under them. There was a patch of matted sawdust beneath each pair of boots. The blueness of the men's faces pointed to death by strangulation. They had been a long time dying, but it was still possible to recognize them – part of the posse which had ridden into the hollow and ridden out again leaving the Cades to their own devices.

The wind force increased still more and curled in under and over the saloon doors. The bodies swung at the ends of their killing ropes.

'Jubal?' Mary called above the sound of the wind.

He glanced around the mean bar-room. The overturned tables were the only permanent fixtures which had been disturbed. Several other tables were spread about the room in their accustomed places, flanked by chairs. Bottles were arranged neatly on the shelves behind the bar. Nothing had been broken. But something was missing – people. A deck of cards from which four hands had been dealt were spread on one table. A bottle of whiskey and three shot glasses – all half full – were on another. The chairs had been pushed back to allow the customers to rise. More glasses, some empty and others holding liquor and beer stood on the bar. Three hats and one frock coat hung from the rack just inside the door.

'Jubal?' Mary's voice was more shrill, holding a lot of fear.

He turned and went out, cracking his eyes against the swirling dust which was being raised house high by the wind as it reached storm force.

'Let me check the store!' he shouted, and moved quickly to the second door in the big building, this one opening between two display windows.

He surveyed the interior quickly from the threshold, then beckoned Mary to bring Andy. Both kept their heads bent to protect their faces from the stinging grit hurled by the wind. It was sweet relief inside the shelter of the store. Mary looked questioningly into the grimness of her husband's face.

'Wait here,' he instructed. 'Don't move. I'll see to the horses.'

He ducked out into the dust storm again, hurried to the wagon and led the team to the rear of the saloon and store. He unhitched the three animals and urged them into the stable. There were no other horses in there and he checked that his three had feed and water before returning to the store. Mary stood as he had left her, with a hand on the boy's shoulder. Both sensed an unexplained eeriness about the town and started when Jubal banged open the door.

'What's happening, Jubal?' Andy asked plaintively.

'We're in a store, Andy,' Mary explained, and it was obvious they had waited in silence for Jubal to return. 'It sells everything from cookies to ... guns, shoes to axle grease. But there's nobody here to sell us anything.'

'A ghost town,' the boy said again.

Jubal moved about the store, noting the comparative freshness of the food and the small heap of cans, cartons and packages on the counter – a half-completed order. Then he checked the two rooms behind the store – the neat and scrupulously clean living quarters of the owners.

'It sure looks that way,' Jubal told the boy, meeting the quizzical gaze of his wife. 'But this place has only just become one. The people just upped and left in the middle of whatever they were doing. Two days ago, I reckon.'

'Why?' Mary asked, afraid of the answer.

Jubal eyed the expectant face of the boy for long moments. Andy had matured far beyond his years since losing his sight and his family. Jubal decided the youngster could take the

72

revelation without serious effect.

'There was a multiple lynching in the saloon,' he explained. 'Four men.'

Mary's hand tightened into a claw on Andy's shoulder as she struggled against her natural reaction to further deaths. Her face was suddenly pale beneath the burnished tone which the weather had given her over the past months. She abruptly realized she was hurting the boy and snatched her hand away. She raised it to her mouth and bit hard on the side of a clenched fist. 'I don't think I can take any more, Jubal,' she said slowly and very distinctly. 'This whole country is evil. No matter where we go, there's death and brutality. It's not fair.'

Jubal could think of nothing to say. Although she was struggling with all her might against the onset of hysteria, she was losing the battle. Everything that had gone before had made large demands on her reserve of mental stamina. He was afraid that one misplaced word could break her will. Then Andy spoke, his voice very frail against the background roar of the wind.

'My Pa used to have this saying when things got really bad, Mary. He'd say they got to get better 'cause they can't get worse.'

Mary looked down at the boy in awe, able to ignore her own torment as she marvelled at the strength of Andy. Suddenly, she reached out with both arms and hugged him to her. She was even able to raise a wan smile as she looked across the store at Jubal.

'I'm sorry,' she murmured.

'You ain't gotta be,' Andy told her. 'Men expect girls to act kinda soft.'

The tone of his comment, which said he numbered himself among the men, blossomed Mary's smile into a short laugh and she stooped to kiss the top of his head. Looking at them, Jubal experienced the same degree of love for the boy, but for him it was mixed with gratitude. For he felt very strongly that had Andy not been present, armed with exactly the right thing to say, it would have been impossible to sway Mary from the con-

73

viction that they should turn back.

'Soon as the storm's over, we'll move on,' he said.

'Like to have you stay 'til help comes,' a strange voice spoke into the room.

CHAPTER NINE

'Don't shoot!'

The heap of supplies on the counter top was exploded across the floor by the rifle barrel as Jubal whirled, levelling the Spencer. The old man in the doorway of the back room thrust his scrawny arms high into the air as his slack mouth hung open. Jubal swallowed hard and felt the warm dampness of sweat holding his shirt to his back. The knuckle of his index finger ached with the strain of keeping it from squeezing the trigger. He knew he was within a split-second of killing the man. Mary looked at his frozen stance and knew it, too.

'Where'd you come from?' Jubal asked hoarsely, still not moving a muscle.

The old man, who was about seventy, with heavily wrinkled skin, watery eyes and a straggly beard, folded his right hand into a fist but left the thumb extended. 'Upstairs, mister. I live up there. I bin sleeping. Woke up and heard voices. Figured it might have bin the gun-slingers come back. Or help.'

Jubal relaxed from his stooped posture and eased his finger forward from the trigger. 'What happened here?'

The old man swallowed hard and his Adam's apple, very prominent in his narrow throat, bobbed uncontrollably for long moments. Although he could see that the initial bolt of tension had left Jubal, the grim expression was still firmly in place. He wasn't about to kill on impulse, but he looked like a man ready to squeeze the trigger at the slightest provocation. And – although he despised himself for it – Jubal knew it, too. He had never fired a shot in anger until the gun-fight at the hollow. But since that night he had felt not the slightest prick of conscience that men had died in front of his blazing gun. It was this lack of any kind of regret which had kept him awake for long night hours, examining a facet of his character which

75

he had previously never suspected.

'Trouble,' the old man answered tremulously. 'These three gun-slingers rode in and stuck up the whole town. Calm as you please.'

'One of them have a scar, here?' Jubal asked, drawing a finger across his forehead.

The old man pumped his head. 'You know 'em, mister. Three of the McCabe Boys.'

Mary gasped.

'Hear the rest of the bunch got wiped out. That's what made these three so murderin' mean.'

'How'd they get the drop on a whole town?' Jubal demanded.

'Went into Mrs. Harmon's house. All the women were there. Hen party, you know? Reckoned they'd shoot all the women 'less the men come to the Harmon house with their hands high. Men had to do like they was told. Soon as they was inside, they was shot. Them gun-slingers just blasted at them like they was apples in a barrel. Couple of the women got hit, too.'

The old man's tone was casual, as if he were explaining the details of some minor disturbance which had occurred.

'Just like that?' Jubal asked.

'That's right.' Suddenly he was perturbed, and leaned to the side, to look around Jubal at Mary and Andy. He licked his loose lower lip. 'Then they ... had their way with the women. Seemed set on staying, but spotted four riders coming over the river bridge. Knew 'em and didn't like 'em. Used the women to get the drop. Then they strung up the fellas in the saloon, shot 'em in the belly and knocked the tables out from under 'em. Didn't stick around after that. Seems they figured there might be more fellers coming and didn't trust their luck to hold. Robbed the dead of money and rode out – heading west. Real mean bast ... guys.'

'What did you do?' Jubal wanted to know.

'Told the woman to go get help. Then I closed up the Harmon house real tight and waited.'

'What about while it was happening?'

76

His hand folded into the fist with the protruding thumb again. 'Stayed hid up there, mister. Guess folks just forgot about me. Never did take much notice of me. I just clean the saloon and help the storekeeper shift the big stuff. Used to, anyways. Ain't nobody left to tell me what to do no more.'

For the first time, his eyes showed sadness. Jubal had forgotten he was still pointing the Spencer. He let the rifle rest on the counter top. The old man lowered his arms with a sigh of relief.

'Real mean guys,' he said again. 'I couldn't have done nothin'.'

Jubal nodded in absent agreement and turned to look at Mary and the boy. They were pale and expressionless: shocked by the old man's story but made immuned to a harsher impact of such slaughter.

'They would be from the posse?' Mary posed.

'They were,' Jubal told her. 'Guess they decided the twelve-way split on the five dead men wasn't enough for their trouble. Wanted more.'

Mary shook her head slowly. 'They deserved what they got – for leaving us the way they did. But these poor, innocent people ...'

'How far to get help?' Jubal asked the old man.

'Nearest town is fifty miles west,' he replied. 'Gun-slingers run off all the horses before they left. Women had to walk. I'd have gone, but I got a gimpy leg.'

He walked a few tottering steps to prove it. Jubal and Mary watched him in silence.

'You're gonna stay 'til help comes, ain't you?'

'I want to go,' Andy pleaded.

Mary nodded as Jubal looked at her inquiringly.

'Please?' the old man begged. 'I heard the young feller call this a ghost town. With all those dead people piled in the Harmon house, it sure feels that way to me. Real scary. I'll go nuts if I have to stay here much longer on my own.'

'Nothing here for us,' Jubal told him.

He was old, with a stiff right leg. But he was light, fast and cunning. He leaned forward with an imploring expression on

77

his wrinkled face, reaching out his hands as if in prayer. But then his arms shot out, and his fingers fastened on to the Spencer's barrel and jerked. Jubal was taken completely by surprise and before he could tighten his grip, the rifle was snatched from his grasp. In another deft movement, the weapon was turned and aimed at him from the bony shoulder. The watery eye behind the backsight showed a gleam of triumph.

'You're staying!' he snarled.

'What's happened?' Andy yelled above the spatter of wind-driven grit against the window panes.

The old man showed a moment of confusion.

'The boy's blind,' Jubal told him.

'Got a gun on you all, that's what. Ain't normally the kinda feller to do somethin' like that. But a man can't see what I see and not change a mite. Just you all behave 'til more folks get here and won't no harm come to you. It's just the company I want.'

Jubal unbuttoned his jacket and pulled out his watch, flipping open the cover. It was four o'clock, but he didn't notice the time. From the corner of his eye, he saw the look of helplessness on Mary's face. The boy seemed torn between fear and disappointment. Jubal sighed as he dropped the watch into a vest pocket – not the same one he had taken it from. He swung away from the old man as he withdrew his hand.

'You won't reconsider?' he asked, his back to the old man.

'I'm trying to keep from goin' mad, mister,' he implored.

Mary opened her mouth to shout as she saw the anger race across her husband's face, taking control over every feature. She saw a burning light in his eyes, the flaring of his nostrils and a compressing of his lips so tight that the entire skin of his face seemed to be drawn taut over the bone structure. She had never seen such a degree of rage in the face of any man: would not have believed her husband capable of generating emotion to such a pitch. And when the blazing brown eyes locked on her own, their expression terrified her into silence. In the short space of a few seconds he had become a stranger to her.

The boy sensed the straining tension and pressed himself

hard against the woman. Jubal pivoted, ducked and kept his arm tight to his chest to reduce the distance of travel of the Remington. The tiny gun came clear of the pocket and belched both barrels at once. The two bullets smashed into the old man's chest and he staggered backwards. They burrowed into his heart and his dead body hit the doorframe and fell forward. The only sound he uttered was a tired sigh as the impact forced the final breath from his body.

'What —'

'Jubal shot him,' Mary cut in across Andy's question. There was a rebuke in her tone.

'Dead?' Andy asked, excited.

'Yes, son,' Jubal replied, leaning over the counter and retrieving the Spencer. 'I had to kill him fast. He had a rifle pointed at me. If he'd just been wounded, he might have hit me. Maybe Mary or you.'

When he turned to face them, most signs of his anger had vanished. The skin was still stretched taut over his cheekbones but the heat had gone out of his eyes and his mouthline had returned to normal.

'Can we go now?' the boy asked.

'The storm's still on,' Mary said, talking to Andy but staring hard at Jubal as she endeavoured to adjust to the kind of man he had shown himself to be.

'I don't care about that,' Andy replied quickly. 'It's not good here. Let's go now.'

He tugged at Mary's hand.

'There's no one to stop us anymore,' Jubal said pointedly, and went to the door.

Mary guided the boy after him and they all leaned into the teeth of the wind, backs stooped and heads bowed as they moved around to the rear of the building. There was no conversation as Jubal hitched the team to the wagon, tied the spare animal on at the rear and then helped Mary and the boy up on to the seat. When Jubal had driven out on to the street, Mary cracked her eyes against the biting dust as she stared at the houses, morbidly wondering which one harboured the pile of decomposing bodies.

The street had become the open trail again before she spoke, her voice raised in competition with the slap of canvas and crunch of rolling wheels.

'You're very adept with guns, Jubal?'

He inferred criticism. 'You never asked me about it, Mary.' His own tone was flat.

'It isn't the kind of subject a husband and wife normally discuss.'

The boy's head swung back and forth, his expressive eyes showing concern.

'Guess not,' Jubal replied. 'It shocked you that I killed the old man?' He nodded, answering his own question. 'It shocked me, too. But he was threatening us. What I did, just came naturally. I don't know if I'd have done it if you and the boy weren't there.'

Mary considered this for a long time as the wagon rolled on through the swirling dust. Andy continued to turn his face up to her, anxious for her to answer and knowing it was not his place to interfere.

'It's all right, Jubal,' she said at length. 'I hated to see you do it. This country isn't how I expected it to be, but I'm learning to live with it. People have to protect themselves and what is theirs by any means open to them. So it's all right, Jubal.'

Again Andy's head swung, one way, then the other. He could not see the sad, weary smiles which Jubal and Mary exchanged, but he sensed the warmth which had been re-established between the couple. He hooked a hand around an arm on either side of him, forming a physical link between the two.

'Pa used to say a man's gotta do what a man's gotta do,' he said earnestly.

'Your Pa's diction was no better than yours,' Mary said good-naturedly.

'But he was a fast man with a cliche!' Jubal put in with a laugh.

CHAPTER TEN

The wind dropped and the dust settled as day faded and night swept across the prairie, unfurling a velvet black sky glittering with a thousand points of cold starlight. But the suddenly still air was laden with a biting chill far keener than the wind had carried. It released this in the form of white frost which layered the ground and reflected the light of a near full moon so that it was possible to see for many miles across the flatness of the terrain.

Mary and Andy retreated into the cover of the wagon while Jubal huddled deep into his fur-lined coat and pulled the collar up around his tingling ears. The frost settled on him as well as everything else and he began to get anxious about the danger of exposure. He knew this was going to be the coldest night yet on the trail and the thought of the store, despite the old man with a gun and many corpses nearby, was warm in recollection. In contrast, the prospect of the next town – still more than forty miles ahead – was cold because of the impossibility of reaching it tonight. So they would have to make camp on the open prairie, with only the wagon for shelter.

He kept the team pushing on for as long as he could withstand the intense cold attacking his face, hopeful of finding, at the very least, an area of broken ground to offer a meagre degree of protection. But the vast prairie appeared to extend into infinity in every direction and when he was finally forced to halt, it was at the side of the trail with the wagon and horses the only irregular feature marking the enormous plain.

He crawled gratefully into the back and encased himself in a bundle of blankets for several minutes, until the blood began to pound warmth through his body again. Mary lit the two lamps and their glow created an impression of radiated heat. He was just about to go out into the bitter cold again, to build a brush fire, when the ominous sound of hooves beating against hard earth halted him. It was a measure of Mary's resignation to expect the unexpected that concern, rather than fear, was mirrored in her deep blue eyes.

'Company,' Andy said calmly.

Mary was crouched closest to the Spencer and she passed it across to Jubal without flinching as her hands touched cold metal and polished wood. Jubal took the gun and levered a bullet into the breech. He turned down both lamps, plunging the wagon interior into darkness, and crouched at the front, peering out through the gap in the canvas behind the seat.

Because of the night's stillness, sound travelled a great distance across the flat country and when he first spotted the riders, heading along the trail from the west, they were still too far off to appear as more than an uneven dark shadow moving towards him. But they were riding at a fast gallop and the gap narrowed quickly so that soon he was able to see moonlight glinting on metal. For several moments the great number of brassy flashes puzzled him. But then the riders were close enough for their silhouettes to show up in stark outline against the sky and he saw their hats. The riders formed a ten man cavalry patrol with uniformed buttons polished to a high sheen.

'It's all right,' Jubal said, sliding out on to the seat. 'Army.'

'Thank God,' Mary breathed.

Jubal dropped to the ground and stamped his feet against the crunchy frost covering as he waited for the soldiers to draw near. There were eight enlisted men, a sergeant and a lieutenant, their faces blue above the upturned collars of their great coats. Curiosity and suspicion showed in their eyes as they regarded Jubal after the officer had ordered a halt. They remained mounted.

'Lieutenant Smart, out of the Fortune Wells post,' the officer greeted. 'You been here long, mister?'

'Cade,' Jubal answered. 'Just got here. It's not the best place in the world to camp, but as good as anywhere else in this country.'

'You pass through Denton, Mr. Cade?'

Some of the men took off their gloves and breathed on

82

numbed hands. Their breath, and that of the horses, was like white smoke.

Jubal looked down the trail the way he had come. 'There was a town back there. I didn't see any name on it. About ten miles.'

'That was Denton,' the lieutenant said. 'What did you see there?'

Jubal's face showed indifference as he shrugged. 'Nothing much. Wind was up and there was dust flying. Just hauled straight on through.'

Smart, who was in his mid-twenties with the face of a man who had spent a great deal of time in the open-air, looked down at Jubal with more than a hint of suspicion in his narrowed eyes. 'Travelling alone?'

Jubal shook his head. 'Got a wife and a boy.'

'Check the wagon, sergeant,' Smart said.

The barrel of the Spencer was ice cold in Jubal's palm as he raised the gun. Its aim froze the veteran sergeant in the process of heeling his horse forward. Ten hard, blue-tinged faces regarded Jubal from under the white-frosted peaks of forage caps.

'You got something to hide in there, Mr. Cade?' the lieutenant asked softly into the silence of the prairie night.

Jubal nodded. 'Guess you could say that. A wife and a boy and some personal effects that aren't part of an exhibition.'

Smart spat and cut a circle in the sparkling frost. 'I'm looking for three of the most brutal killers that ever drew breath, mister,' he announced coldly. 'They wiped out almost an entire town just for the hell of it. Could be you're one of the three.'

'And the other two in the wagon,' the sergeant suggested evenly. 'So get out of my way, feller. I heard the stories of some of the women that got out of Denton alive. Move or shoot.'

He heeled his horse forward and there was a flurry of movement among the enlisted men as they drew rifles from their saddle boots. Jubal's anger rose to full pitch and showed in his face as blazing eyes, taut skin and compressed lips. He knew it

83

was crazy as he saw the sergeant's toughness diminish to reveal a flicker of nervousness. For the non-com knew he was looking down the muzzle of a gun in the hands of a man ruled by anger instead of reason.

Then, as the soldiers rifles were raised to shoulders and aimed at Jubal, the tension reached a seemingly unbearable pitch, and snapped.

'He's telling the truth!' Mary shouted, jerking aside the canvas flap at the front of the wagon and standing in the opening, clutching Andy to her side.

'Sergeant!' the officer snapped.

The veteran reined his horse to a halt and stared down the length of the Spencer's barrel into Jubal's still stiff expression. 'Pretty touchy, ain't you, feller?' he said softly.

'You see any killers here?' Jubal replied.

'One,' the sergeant murmured, then backed up his horse into the group.

The soldiers returned their rifles to the boots, some sparing admiring glances for Mary but most watching Jubal. He stood like a statue, with the Spencer in a tight grip, pointed into the air now. But those who looked at him knew he had not backed off an inch from that threshold a man must cross to kill.

Nobody trusted themselves to speak as, after Lieutenant Smart had used a hand signal to move the patrol forward, the soldiers filed around Jubal and broke into a canter along the trail towards Denton. Not until the sound of hooves on frozen ground had diminished into a distant rumble did Jubal relax his posture, shoulders slumping and rifle swinging at his side. His eyes met Mary's earnest gaze fleetingly as he swung around. She was about to say something, but Jubal completed the turn and began hurriedly to collect brush for a fire.

He felt a deep disgust with himself. Not because the sergeant had spotted the killer in him – he was already aware of this instinct which lurked within him from his actions at the hollow and the way he killed the old man in Denton. But what had just happened was far more disturbing: he had been on the point of squeezing the Spencer's trigger without considering the consequences. Now, in hindsight, he could see that had

84

he shot the sergeant, he himself would have been blasted into eternity by the other members of the patrol. Which would have left Mary and Andy – the reasons for his stand – alone and unprotected in a land which was capable of unleashing danger from any quarter at any time. So, while the ability to kill was, in such a violent world, acceptable to him, the lack of control over his own actions was terrifying. For it meant that only his motives made him any different from the psychopaths who had staged the massacre at Denton.

Mary sensed his preoccupation with his own thoughts and the trio ate their evening meal in silence beside the blazing fire. Andy tried to start the adults talking afterwards, but Mary urged him to his bedroll and she was not long in bedding down herself. Jubal slept fitfully, nagged by anxiety over his latest discovery about himself. When he did finally sink into the depths of sleep, he was disturbed by the familiar thud of hoofbeats approaching. His hands were burned by the frost coating on the Spencer as he snatched up the gun. It was the army patrol returning from Denton. They galloped by without breaking from their orderly ranks of two. Their horror at what they had seen in the town was still inscribed on their faces, even though they must have been riding for at least two hours.

The light of dawn seemed to add a renewed intensity to the bitter cold which hovered menacingly beyond the short reach of the fire. But the first rays of the rising sun shafting across the prairie burned off the frost from the ground and transformed it into mist. Then, when the morning was full-born, the milky whiteness was sucked high into the atmosphere and there was even a faint touch of warmth in the crystal clear air.

The better weather lightened the moods of the three as they continued on their westward course. By tacit agreement, no mention was made of the events which had marred the previous day and the conversation was again concerned mainly with describing the surroundings to the blind Andy. They saw two stages, one passing them from behind and the other trundling east. Drivers and guards waved and shouted greetings. The weather stayed good and all seemed right with the world. Memories when they intruded into the minds of any of the three, seemed like disjointed fragments of a long gone nightmare.

As the miles rolled under the wheels of the wagon, the prairie continued to appear as a flat, desolate wasteland extending to the edge of the world in every direction. But then Fortune Wells appeared ahead, the first disruption on the plain all day to illustrate the earth's curvature. First they saw the pall of smoke from many chimneys as a smudge on the horizon. Then the tops of the buildings came into view and as they drew closer, the entire town materialized.

It was much larger than Denton and the community was spread over a wide area. Spur trails sheered off the main one towards outlying farmhouses standing amid ploughed fields and pastures with grazing cattle. The town at the centre had two cross streets lined with two storey buildings, most of them brick built. There was a hotel, a court house, marshal's office, half a dozen stores and two saloons. The army post, which seemed large enough to garrison about fifty soldiers was at the end of the street which ran north and became a trail across the prairie in that direction. The flag above the arched gateway in the stockade wall hung limply at half mast.

The clock on the façade of the court house pointed to midday as Jubal hauled the team to a halt in front of the Fortune Wells Hotel. The centre section of town, clustered around the intersection of the two streets, had wooden sidewalks and the people going about their daily business had clean, honest faces which spread with smiles as they greeted the newcomers.

'Civilization,' Mary said with a sigh, the single word summing up exactly what Jubal felt about the place.

Despite his dislike for New York, there had been a number of occasions out on the long trail when he would have gladly exchanged the deprivations of life in the wilderness for a few city luxuries. Fortune Wells was hardly a metropolis, but it seemed to offer far more than every other settlement they had come across, most of them as primitive as Denton.

'How would you like a night in a proper bed, Andy?' he asked.

The boy's face lit up. 'If that's what you and Mary want,' he said.

'There's only one thing in the world I'd like better,' Mary said. 'And we all know what that is.'

Andy was puzzled.

'For you to get your sight back, son,' Jubal explained, climbing down on to the sidewalk and swinging the boy down beside him.

Andy looked up trustingly as Jubal helped his wife off the wagon. 'Everything comes to he who waits,' he announced earnestly.

'I know,' Jubal said as Mary laughed. 'That was what your Pa always said.'

'There was a lot of truth in what he said,' Andy insisted as Mary took his hand and led him after Jubal into the hotel lobby. 'That's what Ma always said, anyway.'

He started the laughter this time, and it was a very happy trio which checked in and were allocated a first floor room with a dressing room off it which would take a bed for Andy. When he had settled his wife and the boy into the room, Jubal went on to the street again and arranged for a livery to take care of the horses and a blacksmith to shoe them.

Jubal was conscious that the bills he was running up would have to be paid for out of the money he had found in Dana Prescott's baggage. But he promised himself he would regard it only as a loan; for whatever the Prescotts had left rightfully belonged to Andy. And, Jubal justified, the interest he paid would be much larger than the loan, for the kind of treatment the boy required could not have been met out of Prescott's bankroll.

He had also to convince himself that the time they spent in town would not detract from Andy's chance of recovering his sight. But this was easy. At least three times every day, he had examined the boy's eyes, checking that his severely restricted vision was no worse and always hopeful for an improvement. Their condition was always exactly the same, so he knew that time was not an important factor. It was simply a matter of ensuring that Andy stayed out of any situation whereby he could get a knock on the head: for the cause of his sightlessness was in the delicate optic nerve and there was no telling what degree of further damage could be done by even the slightest momentary pressure on the surrounding tissue.

Since Mary had spoken of her intention to take a bath, and over-ruled Andy's protests against one, Jubal decided he had time for a drink. The Star of Fortune saloon was on the opposite corner of the intersection from the hotel and he had pushed through the batswing doors before he saw the army sergeant and two enlisted men who had been on the patrol to Denton last night.

Had the trio not seen his entry, reflected in the mirror behind the bar counter, Jubal might have made a fast decision and turned to go straight out again. But the reflected steadiness of their gazes seemed to issue a challenge which he felt unable to ignore. It was not good drinking weather, unless for warming whiskey, and the only other patrons were two elderly men playing stud poker for dead matches at a corner table.

The saloon presented a more pleasing aspect than the one at Denton. Bottles and glasses sparkled, the bartop was polished and the floor swept clean. Warmth crept into the furthest corners from a pot-bellied stove in the centre of the room. The barkeeper smiled cheerfully as Jubal hooked a heel over the rail.

'What can I get you?'

'Whiskey,' Jubal replied.

He sensed the three soldiers looking at him, but he kept his eyes averted. They waited until the shot glass had been filled and the drink paid for. Then:

'He sure is a little runt. Must have been that rifle of his made him look like a man.'

The speaker was one of the enlisted men, his voice slurred by the dulling effect of hard liquor. The overweight barkeeper was suddenly not smiling any more. Jubal felt the warmth of the whiskey hit his stomach and spread.

'Another,' he said.

'I don't want no trouble,' the barkeeper warned nervously. 'Two is as many as I allow myself and that's not enough to make me drunk,' Jubal answered easily.

'If Smart ass hadn't a bin there, I'd have trampled him into the ground,' the sergeant muttered.

'Wouldn't have made hardly a dent – a little guy like him.'

Jubal continued to look at the barkeeper, his face expressionless. When he knocked the bottom of his glass on the bartop, the fat man snatched the bottle from the shelf and upended it. Some of the whiskey overflowed. Jubal swallowed this drink as quickly as the first and slapped coins on to the counter. The barkeeper took what was owed and Jubal returned the rest of the money to his jacket pocket. Then he turned sideways on, leaning against the bartop and looking towards the soldiers.

'Are you fellers trying to pick a fight?' he asked quietly, aware that he had now captured the interest of the card players.

The sergeant laughed, too loudly, forcing the humour. 'Just talking, pint-size. We never pick on guys smaller than us.'

The sergeant was the tallest, a little over six feet. But the enlisted men were only about an inch shorter. All were broadshouldered and wide-chested. But their liking for saloons had bulged their bellies, putting a great deal of strain on their tunic buttons.

'That's fine,' Jubal allowed. 'Makes we civilians feel proud that our protectors are such fair-minded men.' He grinned. 'Loud-mouthed drunks, but fair.'

The subdued sounds from the street were suddenly loud in the hushed saloon. Then boot leather scraped on the floor as the uniformed men pushed themselves away from the bar and formed a line facing Jubal.

'Please?' the barkeeper begged, backing up to the shelves behind the bar counter and spreading his arms in an ineffectual defence of his stock.

'That's twice you've insulted the army, pint-size,' the sergeant rasped menacingly. 'First you held a gun on us. Now you slander us. Small you might be, but somebody's got to teach you some respect.'

Jubal could only blame his position on the two fast whiskeys. He had drunk more than his fair share of hard liquor during his medical studies in England. But while he was courting

Mary, during the long Atlantic crossing and on the journey from New York to the mid-West he had totally abstained. Had the soldiers not been present, he would probably have had just the one and left. But an inner compulsion had forced him to stay and hear out the men and the second shot had provided the pretext. In no way did it bolster his courage, but it did, he felt sure, cause him to provoke the soldiers' aggression.

'I need three teachers?' Jubal taunted.

A sneer spread across the weathered-face of the non-com as he extended his arms to the side, across the chests of the men flanking him. 'My buddies won't be needed 'til after, feller,' he boasted. 'One to take you to the sawbones and the other to pick up the pieces I break off of you.'

Jubal looked towards the anxious barkeeper and smiled. 'He certainly talks up a storm, doesn't he?' he asked casually.

The sergeant let out a roar and lunged forward, one arm dropping to his side as the other started a clumsy roundhouse. Jubal saw his move reflected in the mirror behind the bar and did not swing his eyes back towards his attacker until the moment the blow was about to land. Then he ducked, his derby skimming across the room as the meaty fist made contact with it. Instead of straightening, Jubal powered his crouched body forward and the top of his bare head sank hard into the man's fleshy belly.

The sergeant yelled in pain and started to fold as he staggered backwards. He made a grab at Jubal's hair, but the smaller man pulled back out of reach. The sergeant sat down hard between the two surprised enlisted men. The card players grinned with delight.

'Why, you sneaky little bastard!' the sergeant roared, ignoring the proffered hands of his comrades and struggling upright under his own steam.

He came forward again, slightly bent to ease the agony in his stomach. This time he extended both hands in front of him, seeking to use his advantage of a longer reach to fasten a hold on Jubal. Jubal stepped back, weaving to left and right. The hands, formed into claws, swung with him, on a level with his throat. Then, for an instant, he held still, and the sergeant saw it as an opening. He powered forward. His fingertips actually brushed against the skin at Jubal's neck. But then he was spinning in a world of pain.

Jubal snapped up his own hands, grasped his attacker's wrists and fell backwards. The sergeant was pulled forward, then sideways. Jubal fell full length on the floor and kicked one leg upwards. The sergeant was in mid-air for an instant. Then the toe of Jubal's boot smashed into his hip and he was flipped half over, his back crashing into the front of the bar. Jubal released him and sprang to his feet. The sergeant screamed as his spine impacted with the solid wood of the bar. He bounced off and crashed face-down to the floor. There he lay still, blood trickling from the corner of his mouth where he had bitten the fleshy inside of his cheek.

Jubal faced the two enlisted men. His breathing rate was fast, but he showed no other sign of exerting himself. It was the soldiers who were sweating. 'Is school out already?' he asked when the men made no move towards him.

'He looks hurt real bad,' one of them said.

'Bigger they come, the harder they fall, as I guess Dana Prescott used to say,' Jubal replied, drawing puzzled looks from the soldiers.

A bugle call sounded, loud and clear.

'Thank Christ!' the barkeeper muttered.

'That's recall to the post,' the soldier on the right said eagerly.

Jubal nodded and backed off, to allow them space to lift the unconscious sergeant between them. The bugler continued with the call, giving the men an excuse to carry their burden from the saloon with ungainly haste. The card players returned to their game with a certain lack of enthusiasm. The barkeeper suddenly realized he was still in his protective attitude in front of his stock, and he relaxed.

'Christ, mister, what was all that supposed to prove?' he asked, pouring himself a drink and swallowing it at a gulp.

'Myself, I guess,' Jubal replied softly, crossing in front of the glowing stove and going out on to the sidewalk.

As he moved across the intersection, he could see along the

91

street to where several soldiers were doubling into the army post. And outside the law office, a grim-faced marshal and three deputies were swinging into their saddles. They wheeled their horses and spurred them into a gallop, swerving around the corner. The barkeeper, waddling to catch up with Jubal, had to leap out of the path of the horsemen.

'You forgot this, mister,' he said breathlessly, holding out the derby which Jubal had lost in the fight.

'Kind of you,' Jubal said, taking the hat and dusting it off on his sleeve.

'How did you come to lose your hat?'

Mary was just coming through the hotel doorway, leading Andy. Both had changed into fresh clothing and their faces shone from recent scrubbing.

Jubal grinned. 'On account of I lost my head,' he replied cryptically.

CHAPTER ELEVEN

They had lunch in a crowded restaurant run by a grinning Chinese couple who cooked Occidental food with the same expertise they brought to their national dishes. The small room, with its close packed tables, was buzzing with conversation about the tragedy at Denton, and the Cades could not help overhearing that the women who had escaped the slaughter were staying at the Fortune Wells Hotel at the county's expense. The rumours about the number of killers responsible varied from the accurate three to the vastly exaggerated twenty. The latest news was that the wanted men had been spotted thirty miles to the north of town and the combined forces of civil law and the army were heading out to capture the killers.

After the meal, Jubal went to the barber shop for a trim and shave and Mary took Andy shopping. The boy had both grown and filled out considerably since the start of the trip and there was not a single item of his clothing which fitted him properly.

They spent some time – and more of Dana Prescott's bankroll than Mary would have wished – in the Fortune Wells Drapery and when they emerged Andy had an entire new wardrobe. He looked smart but complained of feeling uncomfortable in the stiff new shirt, levis and jacket. The dry goods store, which had a shoe section at the rear, was the next stop.

'For the lady or the youngster?' a thin, servile man asked with a sickly smile as Mary led the boy to the back of the store.

'The boy,' Mary replied, pointing to the shoes Andy was wearing. His growing toes had burst the stitching on both of them.

'I like these,' Andy insisted.

But Mary placed him firmly on one of the two chairs and moved across to the limited display. The bell above the door tinkled.

'Would the lady care to try the shoes on the boy?' the assistant asked, shooting a glance towards his new customer. 'We're a little shorthanded today. Man who runs the place is a deputy.'

Mary nodded without turning away from the display. The assistant fixed the simpering smile back on his face and went through an archway into the front of the store to attend to the man who had come in. Andy, his head cocked attentively, his face set in an expectant expression, stared through the archway. His eyes were drawn wide, as if trying to see a recognizable form in the blurred pattern of light and shade they picked up.

'Yes, sir. Do something for you?'

As the assistant spoke, Andy nodded emphatically, reaching a decision. 'Mary?' he called in a hushed whisper.

Mary picked up a pair of stout-looking shoes which seemed to be the right size and turned to face Andy.

'Four cartons of ·45 shells for a Colt revolver,' the new customer asked, his voice harsh and demanding.

Andy's face was drained of colour beneath its weathered hue. His sightless eyes were filled with fear and his lower lip trembled. For long seconds, Mary thought the boy was sick. But then the sound of the man's voice told her precisely what his presence had transmitted to Andy's sixth sense. She recalled the shouted words which had signalled the end of the horrifying gun battle in the hollow so many months ago: *'Let's go!'* And suddenly she was in the grip of a near uncontrollable terror of her own.

But it was not quite uncontrollable. Her self-assurance had matured a great deal since she and Jubal had crossed New York's North River and now she was able to quell the urge to panic.

'Let's try this pair, Andy,' she said in level tones, moving to crouch down in front of the seated boy. 'I know, dear,' she added in a whisper as she eased off a shoe.

While fitting a new one, she shot a furtive glance through the archway: and could not stifle a gasp. The man waiting impatiently at the counter was about twenty-five. He was tall, with broad shoulders and a long neck which thrust forward his

94

head in an aggressive attitude. Although his face was streaked with the dust of travel and heavily cloaked with the stubble of several days, it was still possible to see the handsomeness of its rugged bone structure. But his good looks had suffered a serious blow and his brooding black eyes seemed to emanate the bitterness he felt because of it. The scar ran for about four inches across the lateral centre of his high forehead: a livid line of dead tissue that seemed to have a shine in the area of deep shadow thrown by his hat brim.

The man heard the slight sound from Mary and swung abruptly to look through the archway, both hands moving fluidly to clutch at the butts of his holstered Colts. A certain warmth entered his cold eyes as they settled upon the pretty profile of Mary's face and figure. It was the kind of expression that could presage pleasantness or evil.

'Here you are, sir. Four cartons, like you asked for.'

The assistant, straightening up from a stoop before some shelves, recaptured the man's attention. Mary continued to hold her breath, desperately trying to recall whether the man had had an opportunity to see her or Andy back at the hollow. But her mind was in the red-hot grip of only one image and would admit no others. She saw with crystal clarity – as if it were happening at that very moment – a mental picture of the tall man lunging into his saddle, with a drenching spray of blood issuing from the gouged-out rut across his forehead.

'Mary?' Andy asked softly, his highly-developed sense for atmosphere assaulted by the woman's fear.

'How does that feel?' she asked, amazed at the matter-of-fact tone in her voice.

'Bad,' Andy replied solemnly. 'It feels very bad.'

Mary looked up at him sharply, aware that the boy was not referring to the fit of the shoe. 'Please?' she whispered. 'Act naturally, Andy.'

A bill was slapped on the store counter and the assistant made change. Mary looked out of the corner of her eye through the archway and the tall man seemed to take hours to check the coins.

'Glad to have your custom, sir,' the assistant said. 'Good day.'

'Sure,' the scar-faced man responded.

His tread was heavy on the bare boards of the store floor and to Andy and Mary the bell above the door had a warning note in its innocent jingle.

'Stay here!' Mary insisted, straightening and hurrying through the archway.

The assistant looked at her in surprise. 'Something wrong, lady?'

'Get help!' she urged, stopping short so that she was in the shadows but could see clearly through the window into the street. 'That man is one of those who killed the people at Denton.'

The assistant had a naturally pale complexion. But suddenly his nondescript face had a chalky coloration. 'How do you know that?' he asked, his voice hoarse.

Mary did not take her eyes off the back of the scar-faced man. He was ambling nonchalantly across the street towards the front of the Prairie Sun which was Fortune Wells' second saloon. Three horses were hitched to the rail and two men, as travel-stained as the tall man, were sitting on the edge of the sidewalk, smoking. She tried to pin down something recognizable about them, but failed. They had nothing so distinguishable as a prominant scar to mark them.

'I know!' she said insistently. 'Get help, quickly.'

The assistant swallowed hard. 'Gee, the marshal and deputies have gone out after the killers, lady. So have most of the army.'

The three men were talking as they broke open the cartons and loaded their guns, pushing the spare ammuition into their belts. Mary glanced up and down the street. The day had grown even colder after noon and there were few people about: a man loading a wagon outside the feed store, a group of four women gossiping outside the hotel and a few children playing tag on the intersection to keep warm. Then, abruptly, Mary's tension tightened into a ball of new fear that compacted her insides: she saw that the barber's shop was immediately

96

next to the Prairie Sun saloon. And she could see through the highly polished window to where Jubal was just rising from a chair, running a hand round his neck to brush away the irritation of fallen hair.

'Do something!' she implored.

Andy stood up, turned and tripped over the new shoes. He fell headlong with a cry of alarm.

'Stay where you are!' she shrieked at the boy.

Andy bit his lip to hold back the tears of frustration and fear. The assistant looked helplessly from the boy to Mary and then out on the street.

'They killed my folks!' Andy was close to sobs, but continued to control his emotions.

The scar-faced man said something and the other two nodded. The three of them mounted the sidewalk and pushed through the doors into the saloon. Jubal emerged from the barber's shop.

Mary whirled around and shot a contemptuous glance at the assistant before rushing to the fallen boy and crouching beside him.

'I'm sorry,' she said softly, suddenly gentle as she helped him to his feet. 'Jubal's coming, Andy. He'll . . .'

She stopped herself from continuing, wanting Jubal to ensure the three gunmen paid for their crime, but terrified of the danger. She moved out of the store doorway and stood with Andy pressed tightly against her. Jubal saw them and angled across the street. His newly-shaved face was wreathed by a smile. But it was swept away the instant he saw the rigidity of their postures and wanness of their faces. He peered through the glass panel of the door and the already nervous assistant shrank back from the power of Jubal's accusation.

'What happened?' he demanded.

'Nothing,' Mary said quickly. 'Let's get back to the hotel.'

There was confusion in the face of Andy as he forced up his head to stare sightlessly at Mary. Mary shook her head, as if trying to convince herself – to make truth out of a lie.

'I thought I saw somebody I recognized,' she went on. 'I was mistaken. It's all right, Jubal.'

97

She convinced neither herself nor her husband. She dropped her eyes from his steady, demanding gaze and her voice was a subdued whisper. 'One of the men who got away from – when Andy's family were killed – is in that saloon over there. There are two others with him: perhaps the same two. I don't know.'

Andy's faith in Mary was restored and he pressed himself closer to her in tacit approval. Jubal shot a glance over his shoulder at the three horses hitched to the rail and, beyond them, to the closed batswing doors.

'Did you tell anybody?' he demanded.

'The man in the store,' Andy replied for her. 'I don't think he believed Mary. Or he was so scared he didn't want to believe her. Seems the marshal and most of the soldiers have gone chasing after the men someplace else.'

Jubal's expression became stern. 'Take the boy to the hotel,' he instructed.

'Jubal?' Her tone was as anxious as her expression.

'Do as I say!' he barked.

Mary flinched at the strength in his tone, seemed about to argue and then took hold of the boy's hand. Jubal watched the couple all the way to the hotel entrance and didn't alter his expression by a flicker on the many occasions Mary looked over her shoulder at him. When they had gone from sight, he made a move to step down on to the street, then shook his head suddenly and experienced a stab of anger at himself. For he had been about to act impulsively again: and to have done so would have meant facing three psychopathic killers with only a short-range two-shot under-and-over to back his play. He spun around and went into the store. The nervous assistant was on his way into the rear and froze at the sound of the bell.

'Who takes care of law and order when the marshal's out of town?' Jubal demanded.

The assistant turned slowly, his Adam's apple bobbing frantically. 'Deputies,' he replied tremulously. 'But they've gone, too.'

'Who then?' Jubal's voice was diamond hard.

'Army, sir. But most of the soldiers left on the same errand

98

as the marshal and deputies.'

Jubal nodded. 'Go to the post and tell whoever's in charge to send some men down here,' he commanded. 'Tell him why and tell him to hurry. Don't know how long those fellers are going to stay in town.'

'I ain't supposed to leave the store when the boss's away,' the assistant whined.

'I'll serve anybody who stops by,' Jubal said wryly. 'Just do it, uh?'

The assistant thought about it and did a lot of blinking in the process. Then: 'All right if I go out the back way?'

'Fine,' Jubal told him. 'Good idea to bring the soldiers in that way, too.'

The assistant pumped his head and scooted out through the archway. Jubal waited until he heard a door bang closed, then moved behind one of the two counters which paralled the side walls of the store. There were a number of guns in display cabinets, both rifles and revolvers, and he selected a Spencer and hunted around until he found the right sized ammunition. Then he went back to the closed door and watched the saloon entrance.

The children's tag game moved off the intersection and down the street. Jubal found himself looking over the heads of half a dozen running, laughing kids. His face became anxious and he was on the point of shouting to the children to play somewhere else. But he guessed the trio of killers would be tensed up and watching for anything out of the ordinary which might signify danger. The man finished loading his wagon and started it rolling. The children divided to the two sides of the street to allow it to pass, then restarted their game. The group of gossiping women broke up from the front of the hotel, one heading across the intersection as the other three started along the street, towards the Prairie Sun and on the same side.

'Drop that there rifle, stranger!'

Jubal whirled to face the speaker and found himself looking at a group of six hard-faced men, one with a levelled Winchester and the others with hands hooked over revolvers. The nervous assistant hovered at the back as the group moved through the archway. There were no soldiers.

'What did he tell you?' Jubal asked softly.

'Drop the goddamn rifle!' the man with the Winchester snarled.

He was middle-aged, with the ruddy complexion and gnarled hands of a farmer. Two others showed the same signs of manual work. The rest wore storekeeper's aprons. Jubal flicked his eyes over their faces and recognized the barkeeper from the Star of Fortune saloon and the barber. He rested the rifle against a sack of chicken feed.

'He tell you who's over at the saloon?'

'He told us who the lady thinks is over there,' the rifleman allowed.

'The lady's my wife and has good reason to know for sure,' Jubal answered, glancing out on to the street. The children were still making a lot of noise as they chased from one side-walk to the other.

'We ain't disputing nothing,' the man answered as his companions nodded their agreement. 'We're just here to stop any shooting.'

Jubal had to struggle hard against the rising anger that was blazing in his stomach. The strain of it sounded in his tone. 'So what do you plan to do?' he wanted to know.

The rifleman sniffed, went to spit and remembered he was in a store. 'Keep you from doing anything hasty until those fellers have drunk their fill and left town, stranger.'

'So they can do more killing somewhere else?' Jubal accused.

'Somewhere else ain't our concern, stranger,' came the immediate response. 'We don't want Fortune Wells to become no Denton.'

Jubal tried to goad them. 'You're just plain scared!' His stare was as accusing as his tone.

Only the assistant gave visible sign of his fear. The others were impassive – to the extent that they showed no reaction to Jubal's taunt.

The man with the rifle sniffed again. 'You ain't wrong, stranger. There's women and children out on the street. Lot more spread around town. Your wife reckons she saw three of the McCabe Boys. Could be a dozen of them.'

'There's only three left out of the bunch,' Jubal insisted.

'Says you!' came the retort, and now it was the turn of the man with the Winchester to inject scorn into his voice. 'You seem to know a hell of a lot.'

Jubal was on the point of offering an explanation – telling what had happened at the hollow and passing on the story he had heard from the old man at Denton. But a glance at the hard faces of the men told him it would serve no purpose. The reputation of the McCabe Boys, high-lighted by what had happened in the next town along the trail, exerted an influence that was too strong to shatter. He sighed.

'My message didn't get to the post, uh?'

There was a mass shaking of heads. 'No, stranger. Them soldier boys is trained to fight and they ain't done nothing but fire at targets since the war was over. It'd just need something like this to set them trigger-happy troopers blasting at anything that moved.'

'Bill!' the barkeeper said curtly, lifting an arm to point.

Jubal turned to look out through the door panel. The batswings of the saloon had been pushed open and the trio of gunmen emerged. Like Mary, he was unable to be definite about two of them. But the scar left by the small Remington's shot marked the tall man as well as if he had his name painted on his hat. Jubal's hand twitched at an impulse to make a grab for the Spencer. But the group had closed in around him and a Colt was snagged from a holster and jabbed hard into the small of his back.

'Don't!' The single word was hissed, so close to his ear he felt the speaker's hot breath.

The trio stood at the edge of the sidewalk, breathing in deeply of the cold afternoon air as if it had been stuffy inside the saloon. A small girl was tagged and shrieked her disappointment at being caught. The other children raced away from her. The shrieking continued – but not from the girl.

It came from a distance: but was louder and higher, tremulous with naked terror rather than mild frustration. The sound was familiar to the trio of gunmen and their heads whipped around, to stare along the street towards the intersection. Jubal craned forward and saw a woman on a second floor balcony of the hotel. Her mouth was wide, her body stiff and her arm was pointing. Three more women crowded out from the room behind her and expressed their horror in similar fashion.

'Must be some of the Denton women,' Jubal said softly. 'Proves Mary and I were right, uh?'

'Told you, we never figured otherwise,' the man with the Winchester said. 'We just —'

He cut off the sentence abruptly as several of the men gasped. Jubal swung his gaze back to the entrance of the saloon and saw the reason for the shock. The shopping baskets of the three gossipers were tipped over in the street, with the contents scattered. And each of the women was in the grip of a gunman, with a Colt pressed hard against her neck. The terror visible in their twisted faces needed no vocal expression to emphasize its depth.

'Hoped they'd go away without anything like this happening,' Jubal said, finishing what he thought the rifleman had been about to say.

The men looked out across the suddenly immobile and silent children.

'Ain't no one been killed,' somebody said.

'Yet,' another added ominously.

The women from Denton were silenced and a deathly hush fell over the town.

'Stay here, all of you,' the rifleman said curtly, then jerked open the door and stepped through.

The tinkle of the bell seemed to have a sudden power which sent it rolling out across the surrounding prairie.

'Release the women and you can leave without trouble!' the man with the Winchester shouted.

Some of the children turned their heads to look at him. Most found their attention riveted involuntarily upon the three gunmen and hostages. The scar-faced man laughed, and the sound held genuine humour.

'You got the wrong idea, feller,' he said, applying pressure to his Colt so that a gasp of pain was squeezed from the thin, plain woman in his grasp. 'We take the ladies so we get no trouble.'

'That's Bill's wife he's got,' the barber whispered to Jubal.
'How far?'

The man with the scar craned his head forward on its long neck to look at the profile of the woman he held. His teeth gleamed very white in a broad grin. 'Tell the truth, I don't have the inclination to go very far with this sourpuss.'

As the other two men laughed, Bill's back stiffened as he sought to control his anger. 'Edge of town!'

The scar-faced man lost his grin and evil seemed to emanate from him in a visible wave. 'You ain't in no position to do no bargaining, feller.'

The realization of this hit the man on the sidewalk with a weakening blow. He swayed and seemed about to fall. But then he splayed his legs wide and stayed upright.

'Anything you say,' he responded, and his voice no longer held any harshness. It had a scratchy quality.

The scar-faced man reacted with his flashing grin, then spoke softly to the man on his right. His voice did not carry across the street.

'Children, go on home!' Bill ordered.

Those youngsters who were too deep in horrified fascination to hear the command were jerked roughly away by the others. They retreated to the intersection but no further, standing close to the cover of a corner in case it should be needed. The gunmen paid no attention to the children – nor to the many faces which peered from every doorway and window along the street. They were too concerned with putting the next stage of their escape plan into action. In turn, each man unhooked a coiled lariat from his horse, bound a woman's wrists with one end and hitched the spare length to the saddle-horn.

With supreme confidence, they holstered their guns before untying the reins from the hitching rail and swinging into the saddles. The hostages looked pleadingly across the street towards the store front but neither the man on the sidewalk nor those in the doorway behind him could offer help. For the threat of the horses being panicked into a gallop was as menacing as the pointing revolvers had been.

Scarface grinned again and doffed his hat. His companions continued to look mean.

'Been real nice, folks.' This sardonic farewell was shouted. But the next word, as he stopped grinning, was a low hiss heard only by the gunmen flanking him and the helpless women.

'No!' one of the women screamed.

Then spurs thudded into horseflesh and what seemed to be a single gasp of horror swept across the town. Each woman was jerked violently forward as the horses lunged into a gallop. They went headlong to the ground and whatever sounds were made by the watchers were swamped by screams of agony. Face down, the women were dragged at full-tilt across the hard-packed, uneven surface of the street. Behind them was left a trail of shredded dress material which petered out to be replaced by long smears of blood.

Jubal was the first man to burst from the store doorway, ignoring the pressure of the gun muzzle against his back as he snatched up the Spencer. The man called Bill was standing stock still, rooted to the spot by horror as he watched the gunmen drag his wife and her two companions clear of the edge of town and out on to the trail. Their screams had ceased.

Jubal leapt from the sidewalk to the street, landing in a crouch with the rifle aimed from his shoulder. Just as he pulled the trigger, Bill's Winchester barrel crashed down on that of the Spencer. The bullet burrowed into the ground less than three feet in front of Jubal. Out on the trail, knives flashed in sunlight and the three horses, released of their burdens, spurted ahead, galloping clear of rifle range. Maniacal laughter drifted back into the streets of the stunned town as Jubal straightened and turned to meet the gaze of the man who had spoiled his shot.

Nobody else moved – as if afraid to discover the results of the gunmen's cold-blooded brutality.

'It wasn't your business, stranger,' Bill accused.

His voice seemed to release the townspeople from their

shock and several of the men from the store raced along the street and out on to the trail where dust from thudding hooves was settling on the inert forms of the women.

Jubal bit back his anger. 'They're dead,' he said softly, coldly. 'Nobody could be dragged that far and that fast without being killed.'

The steel went out of the other man's gaze and his dejection seemed to rob him of stature. 'I had a faint hope,' he replied, his voice tremulous with emotion. 'If you had shot and missed ... they would not have been cut loose. How could I have known you weren't responsible for my wife's death?'

Out on the trail, the men had reached the spot where the bodies were slumped. Each was lifted by one man and the group turned to head back for town. Their slow, almost funereal, pace confirmed that no spark of life showed.

A great crowd gathered on the intersection, pouring in from the main and cross street. They made no move to encroach any further, fearful of closer contact with the mutilated bodies which were brought to the store front and lowered gently to the sidewalk. Only the differing statures and remnants of tattered gowns clinging to the bodies identified one from the others. For the women no longer had faces. From their foreheads to their feet the women had been stripped of skin: even, in some areas, flesh too – so that bone gleamed white amid the slickness of blood.

Horses approached and the silent crowd parted to allow a six man unit of cavalry to ride through. They were led by a corporal.

'What's going on here?' he demanded, arrogant in command. 'We heard a shot.'

The corpses were hidden by the men and the corporal had to ride up close to see over their heads. His air of self-importance evaporated like water on a stove lid. The colour drained from his face and he swayed in the saddle.

'Law and army's on a wild goose chase,' one of the men muttered. 'McCabe Boys were in town.'

Jubal broke from the ring of men at the store front and pointed with his rifle. 'If you're interested, they went thataway,' he told the corporal.

The troopers craned to get a view of the bodies and those who were successful wished they had not been so. The corporal shook his head in confusion.

'I'll have to check with the major,' he said.

Jubal sighed. 'Doesn't anybody around here do anything without —'

'I told you,' the new widower snapped, whirling around. 'You might have missed.'

There were long seconds of silence, as every person within earshot waited for Jubal's response. He chose actions before words. A crow took flight from the roof of the Prairie Sun saloon. Jubal moved two steps sideways, to take him clear of the corporal's horse, and snapped the Spencer up to his shoulder. The rifle exploded sound into the silence. Jubal pumped the action, fired again, pumped and fired. The shots merged into a single report. The crow was dropped by the first bullet. The second flung the dead bird against the front of the saloon. The third tossed the falling carcase over the batswing doors and into the interior.

Jubal swung around and tossed the rifle to the store assistant. 'Like a man I once knew would likely have said, in a different context,' Jubal told Bill. 'Might is right.'

He moved around the group of horse-soldiers and walked towards the intersection. The crowd parted to allow him through, then watched him out of sight into the hotel.

'He sure can shoot a rifle,' a man said in awe.

Bill sniffed. 'Feller built as small as he is just got to have something going for him,' he said cynically.

'Shooting ain't all,' the barkeeper from the Star of Fortune saloon countered knowledgeably.

CHAPTER TWELVE

After the corporal had reported to his commanding officer on the events of the afternoon, a token search and capture force was sent in the wake of the escaping gunmen. Jubal, Mary and Andy met the soldiers at mid-morning on the following day. The Cades and the boy were three hours from Fortune Wells, having pulled out of town just after dawn to the accompaniment of a mournful death knell to mark the interment of the three dead women.

The twelve-man patrol, led by a shave-tail captain shared coffee with the travellers and were not anxious to return to the post. For although they had picked up sign of the fugitives and followed it for most of the night, the trail had gone cold. The mission had been a failure.

Once clear of Fortune Wells, Jubal and Mary had been able to push into the backs of their minds the memories of what had happened there. But the dejection of the soldiers infected them with melancholy again and as they continued on their journey, the troopers cantering off in the opposite direction, the absence of conversation aboard the trundling wagon had an oppressive quality.

'How did you learn to shoot like that, Jubal?' Mary asked suddenly.

Andy had badgered her for details of what had happened out on the street and his young face showed as much curiosity as hers while they waited for Jubal to answer.

'Chicago, of all places,' he said at length, his face creased by a frown of recollection. It wasn't really all that difficult to remember: once he had overcome the self-imposed block he had erected against the events of his mainly unhappy childhood and youth. 'The foundling home was in a big old house near the lake. One day – I guess we were about ten – the friend who left me the Spencer found a way into a basement under the kitchens. He was too frightened to go in himself, so I went with him. It had been used as a store at one time and there were piles of junk all over the place. But we made one real find – an old Nathan Starr flintlock and crates of powder and shot.' The familiar smile, no longer so youthful since he had grown the moustache, spread across his face as the memory flooded back. 'We both thought it would explode when we fired it, but it didn't. And the basement was so deep that nobody in the home heard us.'

'Gee,' Andy breathed.

Jubal ruffled his blond hair. 'Once we knew the gun worked and nobody could hear us, we went down there every chance we got. We had to steal some candles for light, but there was plenty of stuff to use for targets. Took us a long time to get the hang of it. For a while, the recoil used to send us flying backwards and we almost always only hit the ceiling. But we learned. Pretty soon we considered ourselves the best shots in Chicago.'

'Gee, that must have been fun,' the boy said in admiration.

'What would your father have said if he had heard that story Andy?' Mary posed.

The youngster pondered, frowning. Then he grinned. 'I know! Boys will be boys.'

Mary laughed. 'Maybe.'

Andy swung around to face Jubal again. 'But you couldn't learn to fire a flintlock fast,' he pointed out.

'That's right,' Jubal agreed. 'But that friend of mine I learned to shoot with – he was a casualty in the war. Among a few other things, he left me a Spencer repeating rifle.'

'Were you in the war?' Andy wanted to know.

Jubal's expression saddened, but he kept his voice pitched at the same tone. 'No, son. I was a long way off. I'd never touched a gun since I left the orphanage until that Spencer arrived for me. I hadn't met Mary then and the guy who was killed was the only real friend I'd ever had. His death made me feel bad and I got this crazy idea to avenge him. So I started to shoot again. But then the war ended.'

Andy thought about this for a long time, then nodded emphatically as he reached a decision. His voice had an earnestness which sounded strange coming from one so young. 'That was tough, Jubal. But I'm glad those three gun-slingers are still loose. Soon as I can see, I'm going to learn to shoot as good as you. Then I'm going to avenge my folks.'

'Andy!' Mary said, shocked.

Jubal shook his head quickly and raised a finger to his lips. Andy was so deeply engrossed in the excitement of his own thoughts, he did not even hear Mary's exclamation. That night, when Andy was sleeping soundly in his bedroll, Jubal explained the reason for his actions. His view was that, in any illness, recovery was dependent to a large extent upon the will of the patient to get well. Naive and misguided though Andy's motives were, they were nonetheless strong and as such would stand him in good stead when his treatment started. Mary understood this reasoning, for she had often heard her father expound the same theory about willpower and, she suspected, Jubal had probably formed his opinion from listening to her father.

The first snow of winter fell when they were still several days travelling from the Mississippi. It came in the night, falling gently with no wind to drive it into drifts and covered the ground to a depth of about six inches. The morning dawned bright with a right sun that offered no warmth to melt the snow but at least promised a day when no more would fall. The only difficulty it presented was to conceal the trail and for several hours Jubal had to use the sun as a reference point to steer a westward course across the plains. But as the morning wore on, the wagon wheels and team's hooves inscribing a continuous scar across the sparkling white carpet of snow, a line of blue hills came into view along the horizon ahead. And at its centre was a ridge higher than the others and this provided an easily identifiable landmark.

The hills stayed in sight until an hour or so after the midday stop for a meal. Then they became shrouded in heavy cloud, which Jubal thought was probably another snow fall. But a closer, more attractive point of reference had emerged

109

then, in the shape of the buildings of a town. The grey smoke from chimneys and the dark wood of walls was a welcome relief amid the infinity of dazzling whiteness all around. At last Mary had something to describe to the inquisitive boy as Jubal slapped the reins across the backs of the team, urging them into a quicker pace.

The day-long snow glare had not left the couple unaffected and they were within a few hundred yards of the settlement before they were able to isolate details and realise something was wrong. At the town marker, protruding from the snow to proclaim: IBERIA – population 310, Jubal hauled on the reins and applied the brake. The wagon slithered several feet, pushing the team before it, then stopped.

While Mary continued to describe the scene to Andy, Jubal surveyed it for himself. Like Fortune Wells, Iberia was built along two cross streets with the business premises concentrated at the centre and private houses straggling out into the country in four directions. But Iberia showed nothing like the normalcy which had greeted the travellers on arrival in Fortune Wells. For the streets were deserted, the citizens gathered into two groups at each end of the main thoroughfare. Together with a great many horses, the men, women and children were sheltered behind barricades formed of tipped over flatbed wagons and bales of straw. The men, and some women, aimed rifles, shotguns and revolvers through the barricades, threatening a murderous crossfire along the empty street.

'Everywhere we go, Jubal,' Mary said softly, sadly. 'Nothing but trouble. Isn't it ever going to stop?'

Jubal didn't reply, watching and waiting as a man backed away from the barricade at the eastern end of the street and started to run towards the stationary wagon. He was a young man, in his mid-twenties. Like his fellow citizens, he was warmly attired in a heavy winter's coat and he wore a cap with ear-flaps. But his face, with weary eyes and grizzled jaw, was tinged blue by cold.

'You got any ammo, mister?' he demanded, without the preliminary of a greeting.

Jubal's voice was as cold as the surrounding air. 'Enough

110

for my needs.' He had hitched the reins around the brake lever and his gloved hand rested on the seat. The right one was within a few inches of the gap in the canvas through which the barrel of the Spencer angled.

The man standing in the snow held a six-shot Remington revolver, but it was pointed negligently down at the ground, offering no threat. He softened his tone and expression. 'We got big trouble. Three fellers rode into town early this morning. Hit the bank and killed two tellers. We managed to kill their horses but the men made it to the blacksmiths before we could pin 'em down. Blacksmith's also a gunsmith. They got an arsenal in there, mister. We only got what we could carry and most of our ammo's gone. When they figure that out, they'll cut loose. We sent a couple of guys for fresh ammo, but it'll be night before they can get here with it.'

'Three men, you say?' Mary asked.

The man pumped his head. 'Right, ma'am. Real mean. Just walked into the bank and shot down the tellers. Didn't give 'em a chance.'

'One of them have a scar, here?' Jubal asked, drawing a finger across his forehead.

'Right,' came the puzzled reply. 'How'd you know?'

Jubal looked at Mary. 'It isn't us, honey,' he said. 'We just can't shake loose of the man with the scar. He's the one who takes trouble with him wherever he goes.'

'Our paths seem fated to cross,' Mary replied. She seemed about to go on, but suddenly realized there was nothing more to say.

The exchange deepened the man's curiosity. 'Will you help us, mister?' he asked, looking from Jubal to Mary and back again.

'My need's greater than yours,' Jubal replied, the words springing bitterness into the man's face. 'But it so happens we need the same thing.'

He reached behind him into the wagon and brought out two cartons of shells. He tossed one down to the man and kept one himself. Then he jerked out the Spencer.

'This all you got?' the man asked sourly as Jubal jumped

111

down and turned to help Andy and Mary to the ground.

Mary walked nervously, Jubal purposely, as they moved across the crunchy snow with Andy between them holding their hands.

'Andy?' Jubal asked casually. 'Did your Pa have a saying after a harvest when there was just the right amount of food to go round and none to spare?'

The boy's smooth forehead creased in a frown which lasted for several seconds before a smile lit his features. 'Pa was mighty fond of telling us enough is as good as a feast.'

Jubal looked over his shoulder at the man following them. The man was unimpressed.

'This ain't near enough, mister,' he complained.

'You ain't ... haven't seen Jubal shoot!' Andy put in hotly.

At the barricade, upwards of fifty people looked towards the newcomers. Those on watch immediately returned their attention to the street. The others swung their eyes towards the man in the ear-flap cap and showed their disappointment when he held up the carton of shells and shook his head. An elderly man with a silver star pinned to his coat extended a hand. Jubal had to release his hold on Andy to complete the handshake. The boy shivered with cold and Mary hugged him close to her.

'Sheriff Hyman.'

'Jubal Cade.'

'Glad to have you along, but sorry there ain't more of you,' the lawman drawled. 'Ray tell you what happened here?'

Jubal nodded.

Hyman jerked a thumb towards the barricade, his expression sour. 'Looks pretty peaceful over there, don't it? But it was like a full-scale army type battle while we was fixing to bottle them up. Got the ends of both streets blocked off and all the horses outside of town. That's fine while there's daylight. Them critters think it's fine, too. They got the fire roaring and lots of time to count what they stole from the bank. Come night – or even before if it snows – they can get out easy as blinking. Ain't enough cover for us to surround the town.'

'This here feller knows one of 'em, sheriff,' Ray announced.

112

The newcomers were suddenly a centre of renewed interest.

'Tell them, honey,' Jubal said, moving forward and crouching behind a pile of straw bales.

With one eye on her husband, Mary began the story of how the tall man had come by the scar and went on to tell of their subsequent brushes with the killer. Jubal heard her voice but did not listen to it, concentrating his attention on the street stretching away in front of him.

The Iberia County Bank and Froham's Blacksmith Shop were next door to each other, about two hundred and fifty feet down on the right-hand side of the street. Shattered glass, blown out by the explosion, was spread across the street in front of the bank. A body, with the head blackened by congealed blood, was sprawled across the threshold. The big double doors of the blacksmiths were firmly closed, the stout wood gouged and splintered, but not penetrated by bullets. The area immediately around the glassless window also showed countless scars from the hail of lead which had been directed at the gunmen.

When Mary had finished relating her story, the sheriff came to squat down beside Jubal.

'Have you tried anything since you set up the barricades?' Jubal asked.

Hyman sighed. 'Two men got brave and tried to get close. Figured to shoot in through the window from the roof across the street. Hit the frame with two shots.' He blew on his hands. 'Both of them are still up on the roof. One of them did a lot of screaming, but he's been quiet for better than three hours.'

'Killing comes easy to the McCabe Boys,' Jubal said softly, levering a shell into the Spencer's breech. 'They practise a lot.'

'What do you figure to do, Mr. Cade?' Hyman asked as Jubal backed away from the barricade and started for the other end of it.

'I'll think of something,' Jubal replied, squeezing through the barricade on to the street.

CHAPTER THIRTEEN

He was on the north side of the street – the same as the building in which the trio of killers were holed up. And because the building line was standardized along the entire block from town limits to intersection the three had no way of knowing about his approach. But he sensed many pairs of eyes watching his progress as he walked, rifle angled across his chest, close to the house fronts. The barricades blocking off each end of the main street seemed to be straining under the weight of citizenry pressing for a safe vantage point.

Initially there was no sidewalk, the doors and windows of the houses opening directly on to the snow-covered street. Some of the doors were, in fact, open and as Jubal glanced inside the houses, he saw the signs of hasty vacation – half-eaten breakfasts, burned pots on long dead fires, furniture moved for cleaning with dust still on the floor. He recalled the similar signs that had been left in the saloon at Denton.

The surface of the street also provided clues to the panic which had gripped Iberia – snow churned up by racing wheels, beating hooves and running feet. The sun was now well advanced on its declining arc towards the western horizon, seemingly pushed on its way by the power of the biting air which had crusted the disturbed snow with ice. Although Jubal trod lightly, each step produced a faint crunch, amplified out of all proportion by the tense silence.

Then he reached the sidewalk, which started in front of the barber's shop. It was roofed and spread with just a light powdering of snow which looked more like dawn frost as the freezing air iced it with a million crystals. Jubal adopted a slithering gait across the new surface and it cut down the noise he made.

There was a run of some fifty feet of unbroken planking, stretching from the barber's, across the front of a drapery and ending at the far side of the Iberia Saloon-Hotel. Then there was a broad alley across which stood the Iberia County Bank with its own stretch of sidewalk before it. From such close range, Jubal could see the dead, staring eyes of the teller slumped across the threshold of the bank. They were bright blue against the dark, crusted blood which had spilled from bullet holes in his forehead and cheek. Beyond the bank, and separated from it by another broad alley, was the blacksmith's shop.

Jubal held still for several moments, considering the possibilities, then swung forward into the alley which put the bulkiness of the bank building between himself and the blacksmiths.

Thwack!

As he reached the rear, wood splinters spat at him from the angle of the building and he jerked back. He heard the whine of the bullet, then the report of the rifle shot. His lips formed a curse, but he didn't utter it. The shot had come from further away than the blacksmith's shop: one of the townspeople guarding the north exit from Iberia had seen him and mistaken him for a McCabe gang member.

Jubal went down into a crouch and inched forward. A fast glance showed him the back lots of the buildings straggling northwards from the intersection. Sunlight glinted on the barrel of the rifle which had been fired and he quickly ducked back into cover. This time the curse came, hissed low. It was an eventuality he should have allowed for and his anger was directed inwards – at the impulse which had sent him impetuously through the barricade without arranging for the citizens at the three other street blocks to be instructed to hold their fire.

But then, as if fate had become contrite at dealing him so many tragic blows on the long trail from New York, he was given some luck. There was a familiar, raucous laugh from the blacksmith's shop, followed by a burst of rapid rifle fire that sent a hail of lead towards the man who had exploded the first shot. The killers thought it had been fired at them.

Covered from such an unlikely source, Jubal flung himself around the rear corner of the bank and dashed across the back

115

of the building and into the alley. The fusillade of shots occupied both the McCabe Boys and the townspeople and the barrage of noise covered the crunch of Jubal's footfalls.

In the alley between the bank and the blacksmith's shop there was a broken down, once-covered wagon. Its off-side rear wheel was off and it canted at a shallow angle, the skeletonal canvas supports curving up to rest against the side of the building where the three killers had taken refuge.

Jubal had clambered up on to the wagon before the recognizable voice of scarface called a halt to the shooting.

'They're just letting us know they're still out there, the lunkheads,' the killer announced.

Boots scraped on bare floorboards.

'You want me to stay here?'

'Sure thing, Russ,' scarface replied. 'There might still be some hero types out there figure they can creep up on us.'

By standing on the side of the wagon, Jubal was able to reach up and rest the Spencer against the angle of the blacksmith's shop roof. Then, with his middle finger against the muzzle he managed to push the rifle high enough so that it slid past its centre of gravity and it plopped down across the roof, the barrel projecting out over the edge.

Getting aloft himself was more difficult, because of the necessity to get up there silently. Again, the men inside gave him involuntary help, their conversation masking the slight, unavoidable sounds of his progress.

'You know something, Lloyd?' scarface said.

Jubal placed a foot in the vee formed by the wall and a curving support.

'What?'

Jubal gripped the iced support in a gloved hand.

'Those females in Fortune Wells were a real drag.'

All three laughed. The support creaked as Jubal hauled himself up out of the bed of the wagon.

'Kinda funny.' It was the man on watch at the rear – Russ.

Jubal now had the height to get a firm grip on the edge of the roof – once he had brushed the snow away.

'What is?'

116

Jubal hooked one hand in place, then swung his body around, releasing his grip on the support to transfer it to the roof.

'Fortune Wells was the first town we been in for a long time without pulling nothing – and we got spotted.'

Jubal summoned up every ounce of strength and directed it to his shoulders. His teeth gritted together – loud in his own head – and hauled himself upwards.

'Those Denton dames!' scarface rasped bitterly. 'We shoulda blasted 'em.'

Jubal lowered his chest to the roof and wriggled into a more secure position, hoisting a leg and levering with his knee. He snatched up the Spencer and rolled on to his back. He breathed deeply.

'We already give 'em a fate worse than death,' Lloyd pointed out, and the comment was greeted with another burst of laughter.

'They sure weren't very live ones!' scarface cut into the merriment, and generating more.

Jubal rolled over on to his belly again and, with the Spencer held out in front of him in both hands, he used his elbows to lever himself to the chimney. Smoke rose from it in a seemingly solid column for several feet before an air current disintegrated it into a smudge. It was grey, specked with black soot particles.

He had remained below the roof line until now, but had to raise himself to accomplish the next phase in his plan. He got to his feet slowly, the Spencer still gripped in both hands, and he pushed it high above his head as he turned in a full circle showing himself to the citizens at all four barricades. Startled conversation drifted in to him as a low buzz like that from an unseen insect. No gunshots sounded. He saw the stiff, frozen bodies of the two men atop the roof across the street. If he had needed further encouragement to take care, their blood-crusted heads would have provided it.

He stopped to rest the rifle on the snow, then took out the carton of shells from his pocket. He extracted a handful and left them beside the rifle. Then he took off his fur-lined coat.

The meagre warmth from the smoking chimney did nothing to alleviate the icy bite of late afternoon air which cut through his suit to freeze the sweat of tension to his skin.

Once more, he became aware of the many watching eyes which followed his every move. Below, scarface, Russ and Lloyd continued their conversation in a mixture of good humour and bitterness. But he no longer listened. He studied the chimney for a moment, then nodded. It had a diameter of about six inches, which was ideal for his purpose.

He arranged his coat so that both sleeves were together, then picked up the pile of loose bullets. Leaning back from the rising smoke, he dropped the shells down the stack, then jammed the coat sleeves into the aperture. The disturbed smoke billowed, smearing his face with soot. He threw the bulk of the coat over the stack and lunged away, snatching up the Spencer.

'Jesus Christ!' a voice cried below.

Somebody was hit by a burst of coughing.

'The goddamn roof!' scarface roared, punctuating the warning with a shot.

But the top of the building was as strong as its doors and the bullet did not penetrate. Jubal was on his belly again, elbowing his way towards the rear. From the corner of his eye he saw a few wisps of smoke escaping around the blockage in the chimney. But much more was billowing from the front and rear of the building, finding a way through windows and the cracks around the doors. An upsurge of violent coughing from within the building, interspersed with shouted curses, indicated that more than enough was trapped to achieve Jubal's purpose.

Then the bullets he dropped down the chimney stack went off like powerful firecrackers. The men roared and screamed – perhaps in fearful surprise. But at least one of the men was giving vent to pain. He burst out into the open through the glassless rear window, his shirt and hair blazing from where the exploding fire had showered flaming embers across the shop. He pitched himself headlong into the snow and rolled, thrashing his arms and legs. The flames were extinguished with a moist, hissing sound – but not before the fire had seared agonizingly across his back and head. Yellow blisters rose from the blackened flesh.

By reflex action, he had held on to his rifle and the danger represented by the figure of Jubal on the roof over-rode his pain. He flung himself into a sitting position, aiming the rifle. Jubal shot him in the head, the bullet smashing through the bridge of his nose and angling down into his throat. The impact sent him out full length again, with a great gout of blood fountaining from his mouth to leave a red zig-zag across the snow.

As the sound of the shot rolled away across the plains, a roar of triumph rose from the groups at each side of the town. Through the drifting smoke pouring from the building beneath him, Júbal saw those who had been manning the northern barricade break from cover and swarm towards him.

Then rifle fire burst from the street in front of the blacksmith's shop and he rose and whirled. He ran a few paces and flung himself down full length again, pointing the Spencer over the edge of the roof at the front. In the moment before a cloud of smoke rose to obscure his view, Jubal saw that scarface and his surviving companion had swung wide the doors and were dashing across the street, firing along the street as they went. A crowd was approaching from each direction.

Jubal fired through the smoke. A man screamed and Jubal went up into a crouch, steadied himself and launched into a leap. He hit the snow clear of the smoke and saw a man slumped into an inert heap three feet short of the far sidewalk. Blood blossomed into an ever-widening circle from a hole in his back. A second man was on the sidewalk, reaching for the handle of the door to the sheriff's office and gaolhouse.

Jubal, his legs bent to soften the impact of landing and his body stooped, fired the Spencer. The man's hat skimmed from his head and he whirled, levelling a Winchester. The scar was whiter than the snow. Jubal fired again. The bullet gouged a long strip of flesh from the back of the man's right hand. The rifle clattered to the sidewalk and his arms went high in surrender. Behind Jubal, the exploded fire inside the blacksmith's

119

shop took hold on the structure of the building and began to roar.

Scarface's teeth flashed in a smile. 'You made things too hot for me, mister,' he said.

'Hotter still where you're headed,' Jubal told him, altering the aim of the Spencer to draw a bead on the man's heart.

CHAPTER FOURTEEN

'He'll get there at the end of a rope!' Sheriff Hyman shouted.

During the short exchange, Jubal had completely forgotten the context in which he had captured the scarfaced man who, he was sure, was the catalyst of all the ill luck that had dogged Mary and himself since their arrival in the United States. He was within a split second of killing the grinning man when the sheriff's voice intruded into the private world of vengeance.

The sound of the voice was enough to halt the pressure of Jubal's finger on the trigger. Then the lawman stepped into the firing line, his back to Jubal as he levelled a revolver at the last of the McCabe Boys.

Jubal looked to left and right, at the cold-pinched, relieved faces of the crowd, and felt an enormous gratitude towards the elderly sheriff – who had kept him from killing a helpless man. Had he been allowed to complete the act, Jubal knew that a scar would have been left on his mind that would have marked him far more prominently than the killer's sign of violence.

'Folk of Iberia are obliged to you, mister,' the sheriff said. 'But we'll take over from here.'

Jubal was looking for Mary and the boy among the crowd on his left, but the citizens were pressing forward in a tight-packed group for a close look at a man who had brought so much suffering to their midst. He couldn't see them in the throng.

The sheriff took slow paces towards the killer. The scarfaced man, his hand dripping blood, continued to grin. He made the move of a man with nothing to lose. One moment he was standing with an easy nonchalance. Then he made a forward lunge, the grin wiped away by a glower of pure evil. Hyman fired and missed. Women screamed and there was no chance of another shot.

There was a flurry of terrified movement as the killer's weight smashed through the crowd. Both Jubal and Hyman swung their guns. The people scattered, some half falling as others pushed.

Wheels crunched on frozen snow and horses snorted as they sniffed the smoke from the burning blacksmith's shop. The crowd into which the scarfaced man had leapt had become split into small groups, all of them staring in terror at his face, spread with the familiar grin. But neither Jubal nor Hyman, nor any other man with a bullet in his gun breech, dared to fire.

Jubal remembered the man named Bill who had spoiled his shot at Fortune Wells. Then he was struck by the futile thought thought that the scarfaced man was not very original in his escape plans.

'What's happening?' Andy asked plaintively.

Mary was too terrified to answer him. Just as she held the boy tight against her with her hands on his shoulder, back to her legs, so the man with the scar had a grip on her. But his was with a forearm locked around her throat, dripping blood from his injured hand on to her dress bodice. In his good hand was a Bowie knife, the point denting the skin of her neck without puncturing it.

'Stick around undertaker!' the killer called as the hearse was pulled to a halt behind the crowd on Jubal's right. 'Unless I get what I want, there'll be two more for the cold ground – the lady, and me, I guess.'

'Run, Andy!' Mary managed to shriek, lifting her hands and then pushing the sightless boy away from her.

The movement sank the point of the knife and a trickle of blood coursed down her skin. Andy was forced to take a few faltering steps, then slipped on the icy ground.

'Jubal!' he cried as he fell.

Jubal was torn between watching his wife and the killer and helping the boy. A young woman rushed forward, scooped up the boy and backed away. He struggled in her arms, calling first for Jubal, then Mary.

'You're all right, Andy!' Jubal called a reply. 'We just got us some more trouble, that's all.'

Andy ceased to struggle. Suddenly, incongruously, he voiced another of his father's sayings: 'Never rains but it pours, Jubal.'

There was a nervous giggle from the back of the crowd. Mary began to weep.

'What do you want?' Jubal asked.

'Horse, saddled and ready to leave.'

'Get him one,' Jubal instructed. 'Make sure there's no lariat on the saddle.'

'Hey, you heard about Fortune Wells?' the scarfaced man said, brightening his grin. He flicked his eyes down to look at Mary. 'This one's prettier than the old biddy got me out of that town. Yours, feller?'

Jubal didn't answer. He was weighing up the chances of a shot. The man was several inches taller than Mary and Jubal knew he could kill him easily. But the knife could be plunged in to the hilt before the bullet reached him. So, Jubal decided, like the man at Fortune Wells, he was left only with hope.

The young man named Ray had followed Jubal's instructions and saddled a horse – a strong-looking bay stallion. He led the snorting animal forward.

'Keep him nice and quiet, feller,' the scarfaced man instructed, forcing Mary to walk. 'Wouldn't want the lady to fall off and hurt herself.'

Mary had controlled her sobs and was silent, her eyes sending out a tacit plea to Jubal. Ray stroked the stallion's neck, seeking to ease the nervousness caused by the smell of fire. The horse was between the man and his captive and Jubal and the sheriff. He used the cover provided by the animal to stoop, forcing Mary down in front of him. When he straightened, the knife was in the snow and he had jerked a Colt from his holster.

'I'm good with a handgun,' he warned softly. Then, with the ease of a great strength, he lifted Mary in a one-armed hold and slung her across the horse. Both Jubal and Hyman leaned forward as Mary cried with pain, the saddlehorn jabbing hard into her stomach. The Colt was jabbed just as hard into her neck. It was held in place as the man swung up into the saddle. 'West is the way I'm going,' he said.

Mary was as unmoving as a sack of feed slung over the horse. The rider clucked to the animal and tugged at the reins. Ray stepped back. The horse went between Jubal and the sheriff. Mary's head, hidden by her hair, was on the far side from where her husband stood. The crowd parted to allow an escape corridor. Jubal's Spencer and Hyman's Remington revolver pointed towards the killer's broad back. Hundreds of faces, ranging in expression from pity to abject hatred were upturned to watch the rider and his captive. Then the horse was clear of the crowd and moving at an easy pace along the empty, snow-covered street towards the barricade at the far end.

'Let me down, please,' Andy spoke into the silence.

The woman complied and the boy stared sightlessly about him, head cocked attentively.

'Ain't nothing we could do, Mr. Cade,' the sheriff rasped.

Jubal didn't appear to hear what was said, so intently was he staring after the lone horseman moving down the street. At the end, the killer angled the animal to the side, where there was just room for him to squeeze through between an overturned wagon and the front of a house. Then he was out of sight.

For a long time, nobody moved, as if fearful to be the first to do so. The single shot was a far off crack, like the snapping of a dried twig in a dark forest: the maniacal laughter like an unearthly scream in the night.

'Mary!' the boy shrieked.

Jubal was plunged into a private world again, but this time there was no one in it with him. He raced like a man demented through the gap in the crowd. The mortician saw him coming and leapt from the high seat on the hearse. Jubal dived into the place vacated and the crowd scattered just as the first had done. The two-horse team, already edgy from the smoke, surged forward in panic as the reins lashed their backs. But they responded to the driver's demands and swung in a tight circle. Iced snow spurted up from beneath the slithering wheels of the hearse as it was dragged in the wake of the horses.

Team and hearse came around to the full turn and then sped headlong down the street towards the barricade. The crowd held back for a moment, then surged in pursuit. Andy's head swung to left and right, a look of desperation on his young face. Then the man called Ray swept him up into his arms and ran along with the stragglers behind the main body of the crowd.

As the barricade loomed ahead of them, the horses fought to pull out of their gallop. But Jubal cursed at them and slapped the reins. They hit the six feet high pile of straw bales and sent them flying. The horses lunged through the gap and the swaying, slithering hearse was dragged after them. Two dark blots showed on the vast expanse of snow covered plains. Far ahead, one was moving, hardly recognizable as a horse and rider. The other – much closer – was still, transfixed on the snow carpet.

Jubal hauled on the reins and jerked on the brake lever. But the horses, allowed to panic and now seeing no obstacle to their terrified gallop, refused to respond. Locked wheels slid without traction across the frozen surface. All Jubal could do was force them on to a different course, taking them wide of Mary's body. Then he jumped.

He hit the rock-hard ground with a tremendous crash, his feet touching first. He covered his head with his hands and pressed his jaw against his chest as the momentum of the leap sent him into a zig-zagging roll. Pain attacked him from every fibre in his body and the movement seemed to go on for ever, accompanied by a raging, roaring sound like a storm-force wind.

Then it was over. He fought against the pain to uncurl his body and pressed his face into the reviving coldness of the crusted snow. When he raised his head, he saw Mary. She was lying less than six feet from him, in the grip of the kind of stillness which is only possible in an unbreathing, dead thing. The gun had been jammed into her mouth for the fatal shot: the whole lower half of her face was sheened with the slick wetness of her blood.

Jubal, his vision impaired with tears, forced himself up on

all fours, and became aware of the huge crowd, gathered in an arc around him.

'Jubal?' a voice called plaintively, and he recognized the tones of the boy.

'We've both got a score to settle now, Andy,' he heard himself say. 'He's killed Mary.'

Ray set the boy down close to where Jubal was hunched in the snow and Andy reached out and rested his hand on the man's shoulder. 'Mary told me something, Jubal,' the youngster said sadly. 'After what I said about learning to shoot so as I could kill whoever shot my folks.'

'What was that, son?' Jubal asked, unable to take his salt stinging eyes off the blood-stained face of his wife.

'Pa used to say it, too. Only I forgot. Revenge never repairs no injury.'

Jubal shook his head. 'A new one for you, Andy. Death pay all debts. And I'm owed, boy.'

He looked away from Mary's body then, into the far distance, where the man he was going to kill was nothing but a speck on the white horizon. But, as Jubal stared across the vast expanse of desolation, the whiteness was turned to red, as if Mary's spilled blood was sufficient to spread a great stain stretching out to touch her killer.

But it was only the scarlet of sundown.